PEN

TH

'A delight – a funny, pair
– Jane Gardam

The orchards and slow landscapes of the Somerset Levels are as innocent and fresh as sixteen-year-old Billy – until he meets Muriel and falls in love. He is a willow-basket maker, apprenticed to his father. She is freckled, tempting and down from London to spend the summer. Inevitably, quite unintentionally, she plays havoc with his heart . . .

'A tender and painful first novel . . . the landscape lends its own magic . . . I am desperately anxious that this delicate book does not fall on stony ground' – *Guardian*

'As cool and sharp as a glass of cider' – John Fowles

Peter Benson was born in England in 1956. He was educated in Ramsgate, Canterbury and Exeter and now lives in Dorset. *The Levels* won the 1987 *Guardian* Fiction Prize and is his first novel.

Z644

THE LEVELS

Peter Benson

PENGUIN BOOKS

PENGUIN BOOKS

Published by the Penguin Group
27 Wrights Lane, London w8 5tz, England
Viking Penguin Inc., 40 West 23rd Street, New York, New York 10010, USA
Penguin Books Australia Ltd, Ringwood, Victoria, Australia
Penguin Books Canada Ltd, 2801 John Street, Markham, Ontario, Canada l3r 1b4
Penguin Books (NZ) Ltd, 182–190 Wairau Road, Auckland 10, New Zealand

Penguin Books Ltd, Registered Offices: Harmondsworth, Middlesex, England

First published by Constable 1987
Published in Penguin Books 1988

Copyright © Peter Benson, 1987
All rights reserved

Printed and bound in Great Britain by
Cox & Wyman Ltd, Reading

The people characterised and houses
detailed in this book are fictional.

The passage marked on page 131 is taken from *Churches of Somerset* by A. K. Wickham, published by David & Charles Ltd.

1

I riddled the stove, stoked it, and carried the ash to the heap. A breeze came off the sea, miles away, a flooding wind.

I stood on the back porch with a cup of tea. My mother and father took up all the room in the house, we hadn't had breakfast, they were washing. The moor stretched out; here and there, rows of pollard willow, the odd cow, Chedzoy's whistle and his dog. Dogs remind me of Dick. Dick and I used to stand on one side of the river, throwing stones at Chedzoy's father's cows. Old man Chedzoy watched them bolting up the bank, and came to see us throwing, but he couldn't do anything but swear, we were on one side of the river and he was on the other.

I carried my tea to the workshop, and soaked enough sorted willow for the morning. Some people soak the night before and mellow their rods under sacking, but they work as well straight out of the tank; besides, some mellowed stuff goes mouldy. I was by the door, staring at a tree I'd planted against the wall, but it looked dead. Though it looked dead months ago, I can't dig it up; I get a feeling that something might happen.

'Bacon?'

'Two.'

'Let the chickens out!'

'Now?'

'Now!'

I could hear them in the coop, scratching at the floor and beating their wings against the perches. They went wild when I let them out, and though they knew I wasn't going to feed them, they bustled around my feet, while I tried to get back, through the run, to the gate. I didn't talk to them, who feels like talking? I didn't look for eggs. I didn't give them any straw, anything at all. I just left them and went in for breakfast.

Eaten in silence, usually, my father slopping his bacon almost damn raw down his neck, greasy and dripping, almost too much to sit by. From my chair I could see Chedzoy in the distance, ducking in and out of his parlour, the gentle buzz and pump of the machines floating in the wind. A pair of ducks flew towards the river and disappeared behind a stand of poplar trees. My mother told me always to wash the dishes before the gravy dried, else the devil will come for it, so now I do the washing up without thinking, though I know I'm doing it against myself.

It's spring. In the meadow beyond the bottom of our orchard, the first bulldozers are finding the ground firm enough to perch on and rip out a line of trees. Chedzoy will find the luxury of an extra quarter of an acre cancelled out when he's down there next winter with a shovel, trying to clear the rhine (a drainage ditch). The roots of the trees keep the bank from collapsing; he gets rid of them and the devil will eat his gravy. Tough lumps on Chedzoy. I threw stones at his father's cows, but I'm sorry for that.

My father sat in a chair by the vegetable garden while I went to the workshop. Years ago, he shovelled tons of muck into the ground, cart load and cart load. On a still day you could smell Blackwood in Langport. The patch sits off its original level like a mattress, vegetable seeds just have to look at it. It's like this: two plants of the potato Arran Banner filled a log basket. He said, 'Come here, pick him up and crack your spine!'

He grew a parsnip for show, Tender and True, two foot

8

and six inches tip to top. He made a hole with a crowbar, three foot deep, filled it with compost, and the seed just saw green lights all the way down. To get it out in one piece he dug a small grave right round it, and treated it like a baby. He washed it in warm water with a lint-free cloth, and wrapped it in a sheet for the night before the show. He won second, but you couldn't eat it, nobody wanted it, and it stank like a fish as it rotted out back.

The chickens' mash has never been flooded because my mother keeps it in a bin, raised on blocks against vermin. They recognized the sound of her footsteps, and the galvanized lid banging open against the wall, and started a row. I fetched the willow from the tank, drained it off on my bench, and sat down to work. I have rods tied in small bundles of 31 cut rods and enough uncut stuff for making what I call a stake-up. I've done all this cutting and tying the night before. I used to soak all sorts, like my father, but found lately I could sit in the evening and save time for the morning by sorting the stuff then. I don't know why I save the time when I only use that time to save more time to never do the things I want anymore. My father moans about it, but what have I got to do now? He doesn't work anymore. His back's gone.

I work in silence. I listen for the pump pump of Chedzoy's machines to clack off. I'm ramming the pointed ends of the rods into a base. The door is open. I can see the orchard. She lived in that direction. Imagine what I feel like. I have a good memory. I remember everything. Clear as a bell, ringing over the moor on bird's wings. My memory. I work without thinking. My mind wanders. I think about people who visit. I have interested women here, watching, from that association or that guild. They are the kind of people who first came when my father asked them years ago, and I have inherited them. He comes and stands behind them in the door, but can't be bothered to say anything, who can blame him? Why he ever asked them is a mystery. They have nothing in common with us, other than

9

the word 'common', which they think we are. They always ask how many baskets I make in a day and say how nice the workshop smells. I have to tell them about willow. They bore so quickly. They always look lost between something they forgot to do when they were younger and something terrible that is going to happen one day. I try to say things that will make them think I've wits, and some things old basketmakers say, like 'Never stand to the right of a basketmaker'. I tease them. They wear work shirts with iron-creased sleeves. They never buy anything, though say they're lovely and I'm so clever. One or two ask to have a go, but I tell them I can't stop. They will crouch and stare at me.

In the morning, the sun climbs higher in the spring day, it flattens the lands so the trees seem to disappear into the blueness between ground and sky. A haze hangs so close you could touch it. I prick the stakes up. I put a hoop of cane over them, and a brick on the base, lower my seat so I'm sitting on the floor, and pick four of the uncut rods for the first group of four. I weave them in front of three stakes and behind one. When I'm halfway round the base, I add another four rods, when the first four are woven out, I weave these out to do the same with four sets of three rods, and bang them all down with an iron. This is a wale.

The workshop is dark, and cool, on purpose. It has one window, facing south, and the door looks west onto the orchard. Herons often fly over the garden and past the window to the rhine and hardly move all day. Then, in the evening, they'll stand in the river pretending to look straight ahead, feeling for the movements of fish through their feet. The river is called The Isle. I got up and went to the kitchen for some tea.

'What you doing?' My father, still sat in a chair, watching the vegetable garden.

'Slocombe's.'

'All right?'

I walked past him, into the house, and filled the kettle.

10

'Twenty to go,' I shouted.

'He collecting?'

I made the tea while we carried on this conversation, which was about Slocombe being tight as well as bent.

'You made me one?' My mother banged the front door shut, I heard the egg man's van in the road. Her smell in the hall; she smells of Ajax and chickens – bomb material.

'In the pot, got to work . . .'

I still think about Muriel. I remember her walking in the orchard. I saw her on the river bank with a book. She sat in the grass and smoothed her dress down her knees. Because it was summer, many butterflies flew around her, and swallows wove arcs the size of storms in the sky. I saw her on a bicycle, along the lane, going to the post office. I saw her bent over a tap in the yard at Drove House, cleaning her teeth. She drove an ambulance. Dick said that was bloody stupid for a girl.

I just did more stake-ups and wales, half an hour before lunch my father wandered down. It's his business, so he pretended to pretend to do something useful. It's a joke, but I don't mind, he can come up, it's his workshop, he taught me, I like his company. When I was a boy, we got into real trouble, here and at other places. He didn't care then, but of course he never had my reasons. My mother has always had him.

'You're quiet,' he said.

'Problem for you?'

'No.'

He sat down with a clunk, his back's gone, the doctor ordered him an iron vest, but he wouldn't look at it. A basketmaker's vest.

'You're quieter than ever, it was never like this.'

'No?'

'Your mother said something.'

'A miracle!'

'Don't talk like that! If she said something she's been thinking!' I didn't need this, I was tired, didn't want

11

shouting, much, so I said, 'I'm all right,' and 'just let me get on.'

Dick turned up, looking for his dog, Hector.

'Found him?' I said.

'No.'

'No what?' said my old man.

'Found Hector.'

'Lost him?'

'Would he be looking for him if he knew where he was?'

'Just being friendly,' he turned to Dick. 'Bring him a cup of tea and it bites your head off.'

'You don't have to tell me.'

'What've I done?' I said. 'You have an off day!'

'Off day?' My father laughed. 'Off bloody year!'

'Right!' said Dick.

'Thank you.'

'Welcome,' he said.

See what it's done to me? They took their tea out and left me alone. A flock of lapwings blew out of the moor, and the sun dipped behind the Quantocks, the sky faded from blue to pink. When I'd finished work, my mother came out to see to the chickens. She threw them some corn and started looking for eggs. 'Where are they?' she screamed. They just stood around, used to the mad woman who fed them. 'You might as well tell me now, I'll only find them later.'

From my place at the supper table, I could watch the road. A waxing moon slid up the sky, a clearing sky, a gloomy evening mist eased itself into the spaces between the trees that bank the rhines. We ate a tin of apricots and I washed the dishes while they sat down.

When I'd finished, I left the house by the back door, walked through the orchard, and followed the river where it straightens. I walked over South Moor towards Drayton. As the sun grew bigger, it sank, the pink deepened in the hour to an orange and bloody red. I could see Langport and Muchelney Abbey. Many of the houses here are built from

12

Hamstone. They were glowing in the evening. We walked this way once, but all she said was, 'There are ten people in the world, and eight of them are hamburgers.' I hated that.

<h1 style="text-align:center">2</h1>

Drove House is on the West Moor, towards the canal and Barrington, to the west of Higher Burrow Hill, south of the leak of a River Isle. For a long time it was an empty house, so Dick and I spent afternoons there. Many apple trees grew around the place, we knew more about Drove House than anyone. We built a den against the outside wall of the pound house, and counted eggs in their nests. We cut mistletoe for Christmas and gave it to my father to sell off our road wall.

It had been empty since the Bromptons; the moor has never been a place where commuters live. It's damp, and many of the other places those people live, where there are old farms and cottages for sale, are sheltered from wind and rain. Drove House was empty for years. The old wash house still had its coppers, the thick stone walls of the house never did become weak.

Dick and I would wait till late, and walk over after tea, clouds laying ribbons of orange and red across the sky. Many things happened there. We played ghosts. We looked through the dirty windows at the rooms, dusty, dark, the views from partly opened doors showing other partly opened doors into rooms we couldn't see through any window. An overgrown elder scratched at the galvanized roof of a lean-to, once, twice, in a cold winter night.

At school, stories went round about Drove House. No one had known anything about the Bromptons, but everyone said he was a secret agent from the war who'd lived there to escape the enemy, and his wife was the sister of an enemy general, who had been a farm girl, and tried to run Drove House as she had learnt abroad. They moved because of the ghosts. The ghosts lived on the upper floor, and walked between the bedrooms wailing and screaming, looking from windows over the moor, staring with blank, white eyes, at the wind and rain of dark winter nights. Anyone who said they had been up and seen the ghosts hadn't; the sight of them drove men to cry for weeks, their breath killed. On summer days, when froths of seed blew around the hazy apple trees, we dared each other to come up on a winter's night. We played ghosts! What did we know? Some summer days at Drove House I see clear as if they were happening now, great bowls of blue and yellow and green, steam rising from the withy beds, the sun glaring off houses miles away. Autumn in the orchards, when they cropped in the heaviest harvest for twenty years, apples a penny a sack, we couldn't walk for windfalls. The smell of apples and boiling willow ghosts. When you're young. Ghosts in every corner. Winter in the orchards. We had to be foolish at Drove House, Dick and I, then, there.

Everyone had their idea about the ghosts. Old man Chedzoy said they were two women whose brother had been white-feathered in the war, driven out of the district, beaten to death in a wood near Spaxton, alone, on the damp leaves in the dark, but the news had never got back to Drove. He had been a botanist of sedges; his sisters died within three days of each other, and had walked the landing ever since. My mother said it was nonsense, and had no answer, except there was nobody at Drove House. She was right about that. She didn't believe in ghosts.

'Billy,' said my father, going to the store shed, 'got work for you. Come on.' We went in the loft, and he told me he knew the Drove House ghosts were mother and daughter, abandoned wife and daughter of a farmer of 1685, the year of the battle of Sedgemoor. The evening it was fought he was at Stathe, fixing eel traps, when the Rebel army swept him up as they were led by the young Godfrey, through the moor, towards the Royals, who could be heard, drinking in Westonzoyland, making enough noise to cover the Rebels' splashes and clinks of metal in approach. It was clear, moonlit, and they were creeping in the right direction when a mist came down and covered the place. They stopped dead, voices, muffled by circumstance, agreeing on the blessing of the cover, but other voices, asking if anyone knew the way. Young Godfrey knew, said he did, but when they turned towards an impassable dyke, the farmer from Drove knew it was trouble, got as close to Monmouth as he could, but the outriders were asking what use he was, so he left them, headed back to Stathe and the long walk home. It happened fast, the crack of the first accidental shot, the Rebel panic, the King's cavalry riding out of the mist, slashing at our farmer, you'll see the ghosts of his wife and daughter at Drove House, you don't want to go there.

Drove House is the prettiest house round here, in sunshine, with blossom on the trees and bees heavy with pollen, a picture. It's the sort of place you see in photographs of people eating chocolates out of doors. It has windows of thick stone frames with lead between tiny panes of glass, Hamstone walls and a tiled roof. Over an open porch to the front door ivy climbs, up half the wall. All the shrubs and flowers in the front are overgrown, the borders are full of weeds. In the orchard, the trees haven't been pruned for years, but crop as if they had been; nobody goes there to work anymore.

A stream runs to the east of Higher Burrow Hill, I followed it to The Parret at Thorney, got Dick, and walked back again. We were seven or eight, he was a big boy. I had the brains. It was my idea to build a treehouse. I sent him off to find materials.

'What about this?' He found a sheet of galvanized in a lean-to and pulled it over. It was hopeless, I told him it was planks of wood we needed. We found old clothes, more galvanized iron, some bales of straw, but nothing useful.

We searched around the back of the house, to the shaded north walls, where it was cold, chill. It was the last hot day of spring, a day when even some birds shut up for half an hour in the middle of the day, exhausted after a spring flying for their nests, and after the eggs had been laid. But no bird would shelter in the lee of that wall, or in any of the places in the eaves; no amount of down could have comforted a nest. There was nothing there, the Bromptons had taken everything but the chicken house. Dick saw it first, but not the possibility. He wanted to rip parts away and use bales of straw for the walls, but I said we'll take it to pieces and put it back together, ten feet off the ground in the forks of the biggest apple tree we could find.

I took it to bits and Dick did the carrying. We found old rope in the pound house, and hauled the sections, one by one, into the tree. Floor, walls, door, window, roof – all we had to do was bang the nails already there back into the holes they had already made. We erected a fifteen fowl hen house in the double forks of the tallest tree, big enough for the two of us to sit in, and watch the moor around and the house in front of us. We could sit for an hour and watch the egg man on his round, driving from farm to farm, sometimes stopping for a long time, sometimes hardly stopping at all, with the leaves of the tree all around like green curtains.

Nobody else ever went near Drove House, or if they did we never saw them. We always had a good view, but in all the time that summer, the closest people came was to count sheep. The nearest withy bed was two fields away. We didn't know who farmed the land; someone from Kingston had taken it but there were so many people we couldn't tell who. The house was only touched when the postman came with a card, and we looked in to see it sat alone on the mat, with the light from the letter box blocked by our heads pressed up against it. No one else came; the house stood like a fortress and we were its siege, camped in the perfect place.

One day, Dick asked me if I thought we could eat the apples, like it was our garden. I said 'Yes.' He bit one, but though it was ripe it tasted so bitter, and he spat it out. As pieces of apple rained down on the ghosts, he changed towards me. I hadn't known something, so now he'd have good ideas too.

My mother asked me where I was playing with Dick. 'Around the place,' I said. I went to see my father, working on trugs for a gardening shop in Bristol. They were made on a spinner, fixed by a bolt to the centre of the plank, with raised ends, so the base of the basket was curved, like a boat.

'You been to Drove House?'

'Yes.'

'Seen the ghosts? Eh? They'll get you,' he said. I said Dick was bigger than any of them and was waiting for them anyway, so they couldn't hurt us. My father laughed, heaved himself off his board and went to the tank.

'You taking me down there?'

'I don't think we're going,' I said. We had been there for days on end, and were going again the next day.

'You got something you're trying to hide, something you don't want me to know about?'

'No.'

'I wouldn't care what you get up to, just not trouble.'

'No.'

A week later, we went down there, Dick, my father, and I. Summer was a week on but the weather windy. We walked into it, leaves, torn from the withies, blew at us, rain flew in our faces, though it was warm and the sun bright between the clouds.

My father asked Dick if he liked school.

'No.'

'Why's that?'

'Because we can't be playing in our – *Yoow!*' I stood on his foot. 'What's that for?'

'Don't know.' I was looking straight in his face, trying to stop him saying anything about the tree house.

My father said, 'What's the matter?' But Dick got the idea.

'Trod on a stone,' he said.

If I was so clever, why did I make sure we didn't say a word when it was visible for miles? I watched it in the tree for ten minutes before my father saw it at all, swaying in the wind, the door banging against a branch.

'What's that?' he said.

'Our house.'

'Your house?'

'Yes.'

'And yours?'

'Yes,' said Dick.

'Thank you for inviting me,' he said.

Dick didn't say a word. His father was rough, and would never have sat half way up an apple tree in a chicken house, but mine climbed up and enjoyed it. The wind blew in the front door of Drove House and up the stairs to the landing, where it blew and rustled the curtains a little.

He cared for everything he did. He helped us down and said he'd bring a better ladder.

He didn't breathe a word about this secret to my mother; but she would never go to Drove because no one lived there. She didn't go anywhere without a reason.

When winter came, a gale blew the chicken house down, and it lay in pieces in the orchard. I went over to look, but night came so quick, half past four in the afternoon and with the dusk, the rain, you couldn't see your feet, and I wasn't staying round there with the ghosts, so came home again.

3

The first thing I remember about Dick is the first thing I remember about the first time I went in a harvest field, stalks of cut grass scratching our legs. In those days, no one grew grass for hay like now, not since the EEC gave money to drain land and rip out old withy beds for clean ground for more cows. Since the EEC milk quotas they've had to sell their cows and are going back to withies, but it takes years to establish a new bed; they burnt their boats.

Dick and I helped a bale of hay onto the old cart. I still have the picture in my mind. Before tractor loaders, they had everyone from South Moor to Drayton helping in the fields. We boys larked around some bales and disappeared into the hedge to look at our scabs, and we dropped lines into rhines and caught nothing.

Dick's clenched fists were the size of oranges when mine were the size of prunes, but I had the brains; something like the perfect combination for the life of crime that never was. He knew it, so grew thick dark hairs on his arms when he was twelve. 'What are we doing today?' I heard him ask a thousand times, over and over again.

I went elvering with him before my mother let me near the river. I'd say I was going nesting but end up on the bank with his nets. It was day time and we would pretend to catch them in bucketfuls, when anyone who knew anything about it went after dark, when we were in bed. Now, big men from Gloucester vacuum them out of the river for the French and Japanese. Elvers always turned me over; I never knew why we were doing it, other than to see animals die.

We went to school, and sat next to each other in Mrs Freeman's class. We thought when we went we would be smart, but there were other, smarter boys, who knew how to make bombs from eggs and mustard. I liked school, but Dick hated going for the lessons, though in the playground he found boys to thump. He was the boy I knew who pinched girls and then they wanted him to do it again. He was the one who looked after the school tadpoles when they got too big, and kept them until their legs were long enough to pull off. He was the one who tied Mrs Freeman's dog to the bus stop. He was the one who said Africa was in Wales.

We didn't only throw stones at Chedzoy's cows but at Albert Sweet's and even walked beyond Langport to Aller Moor and threw them at some cows we didn't know. On the way home we waited for a train over the bridge, but none came. My father said he went to the pub at Aller with a bag of fish and someone asked how he got such a bag. He said he and a mate went to a bridge and he held his mate's feet so he was hanging upside down waiting for fish to swim by. When one did, he picked it out of the water. So the person from Aller got a mate and they went fishing. The person from Aller's mate was over the side of the bridge, the person asked 'Caught anything yet?' his mate said 'No'. Ten minutes passed and still they hadn't caught anything, until the mate shouted 'Pull me up! Pull me up!' The person from Aller asked 'You caught something?' and the mate said 'No, but there's a train coming'.

Dick was big. From when he was small he led me into trouble I had planned. Our mothers were friends, and went shopping in Langport together. We went too. R. E. Frazer ran a newsagents on his own. We asked our mothers if we could go, and meet them later by the bus stop, and if we were there at half past we could. They gave us each a penny.

I had a plan, Dick the fearless head. I could do anything so long as it was behind the scenes or in a phone box. There was one opposite R. E. Frazer's. I said to Dick, 'I'll go in the phone box', but there was a woman in it, with a dog, waving her arms around. People were coming and going out of the shop. The vicar walked by, carrying a basket. He looked as if he'd just heard something but didn't quite catch what. His head was pushed forward and cocked to one side. He wore wire-framed glasses. His eyes squinted out from behind them at the shop. He had a big basket and was going to fill it. We didn't need people in the shop as part of the plan, the woman carried on on the phone forever.

We went down to the bridge and sat over the river watching for ducks and throwing stones. Suddenly, she came round the corner with her dog; I got up and ran, the sun went behind the clouds, I looked around for our mothers. I told Dick what to do. I spoke slowly – though he's not stupid, I wanted to make him think he was – but he said, 'Why you talking like that?' I only wanted him to understand I was the one with the plan.

I told him to go over to the shop and see if there was anyone in it. I stood by the phone box. He crossed the road and went into R. E. Frazer's. I waited. I couldn't see him through the shop window, and he was there longer than necessary. I was worried in case someone came for the phone and got in front of me. When Dick appeared, and crossed the road without looking, and said, 'There's someone in it', I said, 'You took ages. You only had to look.' 'It's not my fault, Billy.' I asked him who was in it. 'R.E.,' he said. We were going to miss our chance, the telephone box was empty, R. E. Frazer on his own in the empty shop, I said, 'Quickly! Get back in the shop!' 'Why?' 'That's the plan,' I said, and was going to remind him when someone came along and went in the box. I looked at Dick. 'You should have stayed there,' but he said, 'Then how could I tell you R.E. was on his own?' I didn't know and looked at my shoes. They were too clean. I looked at Dick's. They were clean. We looked at each other and trod on each other's feet for a while, listening to the man on the phone talk about his car. No one went into R. E. Frazer's. I looked at the sky. The weather was right for crime. The man put the phone down and left the box; I said to Dick, 'Go in R.E.'s and wait for the phone to ring. When he goes out the back to answer it, grab something.'

It was a crime I learnt from listening at the bus stop. The boys said he fell for it. R. E. Frazer had come from Scotland to be in Langport. They said he was big but soft, and didn't know when they'd done it. I knew it was easy.

I could see the outline of his body in the shop, going to answer the phone. I heard it click and the pips; I put the phone down and left the box to wait for Dick. I waited an age, before he burst out of the shop, yelling, carrying a bottle of lemonade and some sweets. He was yelling – Frazer, red hair streaming behind him like the flames of hell was in hot pursuit, waving a club of seasoned oakwood. We ran down the street and up the hill. Dick slipped on the pavement and dropped the bottle. He stuffed a sweet in his mouth, with the paper, and handed some to me. I pulled him up and saw R.E. behind us, coming up the hill, shouting, 'You come here! Thieves! Come here!' waving the club over his head. Some people in front saw us, and heard him. They looked at us and then R. E. Frazer, but while they hesitated, we dodged past, up to the church.

We were in the graveyard a long time, listening for him to come. I took a sweet, and began to unwrap it behind a tombstone. It said, 'In beloved memory, far sweeter with Jesus.' I pulled at the paper. The sun was still behind the clouds. I could feel the first drops of rain on my face. The wind picked up, bowling off the moor. I shivered, knowing we had to be, at that moment, at the bus stop, waiting for our mothers. The sky grew darker; it rained. I looked over the gravestone for R. E. Frazer. There was no one in sight. Dick stood up, and started to walk back to the churchyard gate. 'Stay there,' he said, when I got up to follow. 'Just seeing if we lost him.' I watched him disappear around the side of the church. I was on my own, my sweets wet with rain. I wondered whether it was worth the trouble, but Dick enjoyed the chase. I could see our mothers' faces but not him. Maybe this is how it always was with him, going straight into things without thinking. He came back, loafing.

'He's gone.'

'You see him?'

'Yeah.'

'Where?'

'Saw his back anyway, down the road, walking down the road, back to the shop.'

'Sure?'

'Look!' he shouted, his face against mine, 'He's the only bloke round here with red hair.'

I got a sweet out of its wrapper and put it in my mouth.

'We ought to eat this stuff before we get back,' I said.

'Why?'

'We never had enough money to buy all of them.'

'Okay.'

'And we've got to get back now.'

'Why?'

'We'll miss the bus.' I had to explain everything.

We stuffed ourselves with sweets behind the gravestones, in the rain, in Langport – our mothers at the bus stop.

'So what happened?'

'When?'

'In the shop.'

'He went out the back, I grabbed some stuff, but the phone's been moved. He was out like a shot, soon as he knew it was a box. He had that club on a hook.' If the counter hadn't been there, Dick said he wouldn't be now. 'I ran for it; he was slow getting round the shelves.'

I was angry when Dick said R.E. had moved the phone; I'd heard he was easy to do, now I thought a life of crime wasn't a good idea. We sat with our heads against the gravestones, eating the last of the sweets, trying to keep the rain off, letting the minutes pass. I pulled my shirt over the back of my neck; my body shivered, then two huge hands,

23

their knuckles covered with tiny red hairs, appeared over the top of the stone, and grabbed us, smothering our faces, one over me, the other on Dick. They just lifted us off the ground, our backs, rubbing up the stone, were pressed so tight against it I couldn't breathe. When we were almost standing up, I felt the whole of my body go light, and I wet myself. Steam rose from the ground, and the hands changed from being on our faces to being on our ears. R. E. Frazer was shouting.

'That'll be one and three.' I couldn't open my mouth with all the sweets in. He looked at Dick. 'The ringleader?' he said. Dick always got called the ringleader, said he wasn't, and no one believed him.

'No.'

'Don't make me laugh, laddie. I've seen you. One and three!'

'Haven't got it.' Dick looked at me. He stayed cool. I couldn't say anything. The sweets in my mouth had made a mass of goo and I was beginning to choke. Creamy pine-apple spit was pouring out of one side of my mouth.

'Then your father will.'

Dick wet himself. We stood in the graveyard in the rain, R. E. Frazer holding onto our ears, with columns of steam rising all around.

'Then your father will?' This was a question. Dick couldn't piss anymore. I wiped the spit off my mouth. I couldn't help it and started crying. Dick looked at me. My ear was ringing. If my whole body had been as hot as my ear I would have been comfortable.

'Our mothers are . . .'

'What?'

'Waiting for us. At the bus stop.'

'Bully for them, laddie,' R. E. Frazer said. He had an odd way of talking, marching us out of the graveyard and back down the road. He had one of our ears in each hand. Some people were going to say something about him hurting us, but he just said, 'Thieves', and the people didn't try to save

24

us. My trousers had gone cold. At the bus stop our mothers were walking up and down and looking around. Dick's mother saw us first and called mine over.

'You these thieves' mothers?' R.E. said.

'Thieves?'

'Aye. They stole from my shop.' He pointed down the road.

'They wouldn't dream . . .'

'Maybe not. But they'd do it in broad daylight.'

Our mothers looked at us and asked if we'd been stealing. I nodded. Dick kept still. His mother gave him a slap on the side of the face. He sat down. She was blue in the face. I thought she was going to die.

'Did you steal?' she screamed, picking him up and shaking him. A few people turned around in the street and stared at us, Dick, his mother, my mother and R.E. and his bristly fist on my ear.

'Did you steal from Mr Frazer?'

'Yes,' he said, very quietly.

'One and three,' said R.E.

'One and three!' repeated his mother, 'One and three! That's the last penny you get for a year! One and three!'

Dick looked at me. I thought he'd say it was my idea. He opened his mouth but just as something was coming out I got hit, from behind, by my mother. I was thrown to the ground six feet away from Dick and his mother, mine had turned red, like R.E. who was standing with his jaw slack, staring at her.

'Your father will . . .' she screamed at me, 'I'm so ashamed . . .' and then she shook her head to get herself back to where she was. She scrabbled for her handbag and found some cash. There was a long thing with Dick's mother as they insisted on paying each son's share of thievery. We stayed on the pavement, very still, watched the money change hands. R. E. Frazer nodded his head without speaking, and walked away.

'Get up! And be home by tea!' our mothers screamed,

getting on the next bus, leaving us standing with three miles to get home.

We planned escape, walking on the moor south of Langport, down towards The Isle. Dick did all the talking, saying this way and that was a good hiding place, we could live in a barn by the canal at Hambridge; but I knew we couldn't – he knew it too, I said.

I left him on South Moor, and turned east towards Blackwood. If I had walked three more miles towards Kingsbury, and climbed Higher Burrow Hill, I could have looked back towards home, as the night gloomed down and owls cried over the moor, long high sounds between the withy beds and rhines. In the distance I could have watched the lights come on at Blackwood, my mother clearing the table for tea, my father washing, drying himself, going into the front room for the strop, draping it over the back of the chair and sitting down. In with the cries of the owls would come a different cry, though as loud and high, coming from Little Creech, Dick's home. Sitting beneath the single tree that grows on Higher Burrow Hill, amongst the sheep's droppings, I could have saved myself for an extra hour, but soon the breeze would pick up to a wind and I'd have to go home. Other lights blinked on, shivering in the dark. Below me, there would have been Kingsbury Episcopi and West Moor towards Hambridge, and the ridge of hills with Curry Rivel and Langport. Behind, to the south, the land rose away towards Haselbury Plucknett and Crewkerne. Closer to me, on the moor below, Drove House brooded in the dark. I could have thought about what faced me at Blackwood, the moon would have risen high in the sky. I could have imagined my mother beginning to regret leaving me to walk all that way home alone with night approaching, my father starting to chide her, she arguing it was only what I deserved, a nagging doubt worrying her, 'Is he safe, safe?' I could have gone to the pool at Thorney Mills and torn my clothes and jumped in the water, lain in the mud and cut my legs on barbed wire, staggered in through the back, mumbling about a man who'd caught me on the South Moor, and I'd only escaped by swimming The Isle. It would have got dark enough to lose coal, I'd be sat by the fire with a drink and everything about thieving forgotten. 'What did he look like, son?' 'Have you seen him before?' I could have lied, dreamt of violent hands. In the night, the owls would have stilled, the river stopped running to the sea.

But I'd left Dick on South Moor, and turned east to Blackwood, the afternoon cooling, night falling. As I walked by the side of the house and round the back, the kitchen light came on, and I watched her for a moment, putting a pan on, leaving the door between the kitchen and the front door ajar, so I could see my father's knees in the light. I opened the back door.

'Billy!' My mother. I watched my father's shadow climb the wall and angle across the ceiling, before he appeared in the door, the strop hanging off his shoulder, my mother's face, framed in the crook of his arm. Her face was flushed, she'd been telling him to tell me what was what and leave wide stripes on my body. He looked fierce, walked to where I stood, spun me round with a flick of his hand, and kicked me out of the door with a heavy boot, back into the yard. An owl screeched like ripped steel, he grabbed my hair and shouted, 'Thieve from town! You'll pay for this, Billy-boy.' He shot me past the veg. garden and kicked me into the workshop.

I didn't say a word. He shouted some more, but I got the idea that what he was doing wasn't all he could. Suddenly, after he'd pushed me into the corner, against a stack of willow, he said, 'Just yell!' I looked at him when he grabbed me, slapped the strop against the wall and said, 'Yell!' He slapped the strop again, and again, until I yelled out. *'Eeeyh!'* 'Better,' he whispered, shouting, 'You disgrace your mother in town, you'll not,' (slap) *'Eeeyh!'* 'do it again.'

He picked me off the willow and said in the war, a boy

27

from Glasgow, evacuated to Langport, put mothballs in his chocolate ration. Now he hated the Scottish. He said, 'But tell your mother I let you off and it'll be for real.' He winked. He didn't want to hit me. I nodded. He hit me once in the face, to make me cry, to convince my mother. He grabbed my hair again, stroked the back of my neck, pulled me back to the house, so I wouldn't let my mother see me naked for weeks, until I thought the stripes that were never there had gone.

4

Drove House stood through the winter our chicken house blew out of the tree, the back fields around Blackwood flooded, and Dick and I saw less of each other after school; when it rained, we lost all the better ideas for things to do. One stormy night, my father came in from the rain with a bird, a Manx shearwater. It was dead. 'Blown by the storm.' It had died, exhausted, on a flooded moor, its last, screaming breath, the devil-bird's cry for the lost sailor's soul it hosted, bewildered amongst the lashing withy sets. Dying alone, far from the craggy tops of rocks amongst its brethren, where its cries had joined the cries of thousands. My father knew lots of things, and liked to prove a point. He laid the body on the floor by the stove, and found a candle.

My mother said, 'You crazy man.'

'You won't be saying that in five minutes.'

'I'll say it till I die.'

'You'll see.'

'Don't I always?'

'And don't you always see that I do what I say I'm going to do?'

'Only when you tell us what it is.'

He fetched an enamel bowl from the yard and put it on the stove.

'What you doing?' I whispered, standing on my toes, leaning over to look at the candle melting in the bowl.

'I need a wick.'

'Why?'

'You'll see.'

He turned the bird over with his foot, one of its legs opened, the feathers in perfect rows, a pink leg, awkward, stiff and dead.

When all the wax had melted, and the room was full of an awful smell, he took a nail, and lifted the wick out. He took the bowl away, let it cool in the storm, he was gone five minutes but came back with a length of wire, bent, with a twist at one end.

My mother watched him, and I watched him while she cooked in the room full of the smell of cabbage and wax. He took the wick and tied it in a loop to the twist in the wire.

'Saw this in a book,' he said.

He took the wire, the wick, and picked the bird off the floor. He pushed the wire down its throat and deep into its body, fiddled until it came loose, and arranged the wick so it stood from the beak.

'You can burn them,' he said, 'like candles. They're full of oil. Scottish do it.'

Mother went mad, not in her house, ever, was a bird going to sit on the side and burn. No. No. No. No burning birds.

So, after a meal when nothing was said, my father went to the workshop with the wicked thing; I heard the door slam shut, and watched the light go on. A minute passed. Two minutes, three, before the light went out, and another light burned.

I went to the front room while my mother was in the kitchen, looked at the floor and went back to the kitchen. While she went upstairs, I crept out of the back door, through the storm, across the yard to the workshop. My father was sitting by the window with the bird burning on the floor, its head on fire, throwing a ghastly orange light around the walls, filling the shed with clouds of thick, black smoke, and a horrible sickening smell. Spats of hot flesh popped into the air, my father sat in its light with a shallow look in his eyes, then he threw a bucket of water on the thing and we came back out of the workshop, through the storm, into the house.

Drove House stood through the winter our chicken house blew out of the tree, the back fields around Blackwood flooded, but Dick and I met on a February day, after school, in boots, to walk over. Even as we set off the sky darkened, it rained on our faces, we put our heads down and walked. We got soaked to the skin, didn't see anything, found it difficult to believe that in weeks the moor would be bright and gay, with primroses on the banks and in the sun. What were we doing? We were walking along in the rain, crossing the last rhine by the cattle bridge, coming at Drove House from the north, towards the cold back of the building. The place smelt of decay. A bang. A piece of tin banging under the lean-to in the wind. Against the pound house piled a heap of bricks and wood, and a gate, off its hinges, at an angle to the wall. The trees in the orchard blew one way, and where the chicken house had collapsed lay broken panels and the door, still in its frame, hanging, the only piece still in the tree banging, bang bang bang. The terrible leafless trees, Dick, a yard away, looking at the remains; half a mile away, Higher Burrow, empty of sheep, with the wind whipping the grass into whirlpools; me, looking back at the house in the storm, its front door solid against the weather, the bang bang of the tin under the lean-to, the bang of the chicken house door, the third, awful thud, of a window, loose on its hinges, on the ground floor of the house, banging open suddenly, then shut.

I stared at it. Unless we'd broken a window, and forced

the leaded frames with pliers, we would never have found a way into Drove House. Thud. I could see dust in the room, dark square shapes of huge furniture, I called Dick.

'See that?' I pointed, and the window flipped open, shut. He looked at me.

'Great,' he said, and started walking towards it. I caught up and pulled at his coat.

'We can't go in.'

'Want a bet?'

'But, if we . . . ?'

'I'm getting out of the rain.'

He got up, climbed through the window, and dropped out of sight, the first one of us in Drove House, squatting beneath the window sill, with me standing outside, and then heaving myself up too. I squeezed in, and fell on Dick, who was crouching, looking around.

'It smells,' he said.

I could, I did smell it, apricots.

'It's marzipan, and vinegar,' he said.

'It's apricots.'

He sniffed, and said it was what he thought it was, as we stood up in the room, looking around. Chairs lined one wall, and opposite, a cupboard, with a broom hanging on its latch. A half open door led into the kitchen, bang, the tin there, outside, banging against the outside of the house. We walked to a door, kicking up little spews of dust, and into the kitchen. We shivered, together, suddenly, like you suddenly do, with no control or warning. A pane of glass, loose in its frame, clinked in the room, the cold burning through our boots from the flags. I flicked my hood off, Dick did the same, we looked at each other.

'Colder in here than it is out,' he said, rubbing his hair and poking at a cupboard door.

'But it's not raining.'

I rubbed one of the windows, and peered at the rain, the sky, a huge shadow in itself.

'Dark soon,' I said.

'So what are we going to do?'

'What you want to do?'

'Don't know.'

'We shouldn't be here.'

'Why not?'

'Well . . .'

Bang, the window in the room behind us banged shut, again.

'We should go,' I said.

'You're scared.'

'I'm not.'

'Then I'm looking around.'

'Oh.'

'You go back outside, if you want,' he said.

I wasn't used to the planning taken from my control. I had suggested we come here in the first place, now, because he was bigger, I was standing next to him while he decided what we were going to do. He left the kitchen by another door, into the corridor and up the stairs. I heard him walk into the first bedroom, his boots shaking flakes of paint off the ceiling. He wasn't going to be without me. I ran upstairs, onto the landing. The arrangement was similar to Blackwood's, three bedrooms, you had to walk through one to get to the next, I dashed into the first, shouting, 'Dick!' though in the light, I couldn't see him anywhere. I heard tiny clicks, in the wall, or the ceiling above me, the sound of fingers snapping. It stopped. It started again. It stopped. I rubbed my eyes, 'Dick!' I shouted again, looking behind the door, and walking into the last room, where I could feel the smell, almost staining the floor apricot, but he was sitting on the window sill, looking out at the night and the orchard.

'We should have got in when the tree house was up,' he said. 'We'll leave that window open, for when we come back.'

'Come back?'

'You are scared.'

'I am not,' I said, though I was looking at the way night came from evening so quickly, and I was looking at the door between the first two bedrooms close, so gently, not like it was breezed shut at all. It just stopped there and sat on its hinges, like it knew I was watching. Bang, the downstairs window flipped back again, bang, bang, the tin again in the lean-to, and something else, north of the place, a crack or two in the night.

'We've got to get back,' I said.

'Chicken.'

'I'll get it if tea's cold.' Dick got up and paced towards the door, saw the other door had closed, and said, 'When did that door shut?'

'Then. I watched it.' There was rustling, in the loft above us, rats, or mice.

'You smell that?' said Dick.

I sniffed. Bang.

'It is apricots.'

'Told you.'

'Can you smell it?'

'No.'

Then I did, in a wave, coming from the kitchen, like someone was down there stewing.

'Yes,' I said, 'let's get out.'

He was through the second bedroom to the door into the first, but while we'd smelt apricots, the door had shut completely, he turned the knob and nothing happened. He turned and pulled, but it didn't move.

'Give us a hand!' he shouted, and I took the handle. A squall of wind rattled every pane of glass in every window of the house, the clouds blew open a moment to let in a view of higher, racing cloud, screwing across the face of an angry, waning moon, and then the light it gave was gone. I pulled at the door, but it didn't move.

'Let me!' Dick yanked at it. 'Grab me,' he said, 'Pull!' I did, but stupid, I slipped. In the dark room I lay on the floor, while the wind and rain pounded, pound, pound, and Dick's breathing grew louder, panting at the jammed door.

'Apricots,' he said.

'What's that?' I said.

'What?'

'Listen.'

'I am.'

'There.'

The window banged downstairs, but we heard scratching, like fingernails being drawn slowly down wood, a door, or a thin wall. There were no thin walls in Drove House. In the darkness, Dick's eyes looked out at me, glistening, big eyes asking what are we going to do? Was it the wind or did I hear a scream? A door crashed in. I heard a clunk on the stairs, another, clunk, another, another. Something was coming up. I pulled at the door but it didn't move. The clunks stopped, and there was one clunk back down.

'What are we going to do?' Dick pulled at my coat. We stood in the room. There was the sound of fingernails then, down the door we faced. The door we faced. Fingernails.

'I don't know,' I said.

'You don't?'

'Why should I?'

'You always used to.'

'Well I don't now.' Clunk. Whatever was coming up the stairs went down again. I tried the door, it still wouldn't move. Thunder crashed, miles away, a minute later the room was illuminated by shafts of lightning; an empty bedstead, an old chest of drawers, a dressing table and two chairs. Dick stood at the window, his ears cocked, his face up against the glass, claiming he'd heard voices, seen human shapes, moving across the orchard towards the house.

'You're kidding.' I said.

'I'm not!'

'Then who were they?'

34

'I don't know; I couldn't see their faces.'

'There.'

'There what?'

'Say what they look like and I might believe you.'

'Might?'

'Yes.'

'I'm telling you,' he said, but I told him to do something useful, at least help with the door, when I heard the sounds of footsteps, walking across the room beneath us, and the first of more clunks on the stairs.

'Hear that?' I said.

'Yes.' He backed away from the window, but knocked into a table, put a hand out to steady himself, and grabbed at the curtain; this came away in his hand, he pulled the rod out of the wall, fell over, and lay on the floor. A whine, a whistle, another crash; clunk.

'Dick?' I whispered.

'What?'

'I'm scared.'

He looked at me, got up, and tried the door again. Scratch, scratch, the elder tree at the window, clunk, crash, a piece of tin blew across the yard. I stood, shaking, following drops of rain streaming down the glass, racing and mingling, stopping, falling and spreading. My palms began to sweat, the hairs on the back of my neck bristled.

'Help me!' he shouted, but it wasn't any use, we pulled and struggled at the door. It was like someone had glued it to the frame. We were stuck. It was dark, then light as another streak of lightning shot across the sky.

We sat on the floor with our backs against the wall, I wondered if we could climb out of the window and drop down to safety. Dick picked his nose. I was about to suggest the idea when there were four bangs from the other bedroom, a light streamed in at us from under the door and the door knob began to move.

'Dick?' I said, 'Dick?'

'What?'

A crash, the sound of fingernails again, and what could have been knives, tapping. Someone breathing, a boom of thunder and suddenly the door swung back, light filled the room and my mother stood in front of us, opened her mouth, and said, 'What the bloody hell are you doing here? We've been sick with worry. And Dick?' She pointed at him. 'Your father's waiting for you!'

Our bodies went loose, she shone a torch in our faces, her body framed in the door, blocking it.

'You could have the police on you!' she screamed, scratching the side of her face. 'I left my hens out on a night like this to come chasing after you.' To prove the point, the wind gusted, once, twice against the sides of the house, in blows, sheets of rain whipped at the roof above us, shaking the slates in their clips.

I said, 'We didn't . . .'

'No we didn't . . .' Dick interrupted. 'No.' He could see the picture of his father waiting, so he didn't say anything else.

'We came in to close the window.'

'What window?'

'Downstairs.'

'None open down there. We had to break the kitchen door.'

'We never heard, I don't think.'

'How did you get in?'

'Through the window. Promise. It was open.'

'Lies?'

'Promise. Cross my heart; we did. It was open. We were wet so we climbed in to get dry and close it. We would have told you.'

'I don't believe it; you broke in. Where?'

'We didn't. Mother, it was open, banging, in the wind.'

'So who shut it?'

'I don't know!'

'We tried all the windows. And we were shouting, didn't you hear us?'

36

'I might have.'

'This,' she cried, 'is the last time you come here. Your father . . .' I could hear him outside. 'He's in the orchard, clearing a load of your rubbish.'

I went to the window and saw him, in the dark, like he had almost become his own shadow, carrying a piece of chicken house in the rain, his hat pulled down on his head, while she stood in the door. Dick stared at his feet, and I shivered.

'So,' she yelled, '*Move!*'

We bolted out of Drove House, down the stairs, through the kitchen and out to the lean-to where my father was sheltering. I tried to say something, but my mother slammed the back door shut and marched us away from the place like an army of rats.

I could feel the pulses behind my ears racing, and a creeping on my palms, chasing along in the rain. I looked back at the house. It stood in the storm, as the clouds opened again and showed a moon to light the scene; in an eerie, pale light, Drove House, a pool of darkness.

'Who shut that window?' I said to Dick.

'And closed the door?'

'And got it stuck?'

'I don't know.'

'Enough talk!' my mother shouted; she strode ahead through the mud on the road, between the low hedges towards South Moor, when she left us to take Dick back to his father, and what waited for him.

I held on to my father as we walked back to Blackwood.

'What you hanging on for?'

'We did get in through the window,' I said, 'Someone closed it.'

'The wind?'

'The wind?'

'Yes.'

'No.'

37

'It couldn't have been anything else. Unless the ghosts were walking tonight.'

'The ghosts?'

'Why not? After dark, you shouldn't go there,' he stopped in the road. 'Really,' he said.

'Really?'

'But you don't want to worry.'

'No?'

'Worry about your mother.'

He let me into Blackwood, helped me out of my clothes by the stove, and I was in bed before she got back from Dick's. He said he'd see she didn't come for me. I was lying, staring at the ceiling and the light coming in from under the door. By the time she got back – I heard her pound through the yard and in the back door – by this time the storm had quietened, the rain no longer beat at my window; but I sat up in bed and thought I heard the sound of fingernails tapping, somewhere, in my frightened head.

5

As I sit here at Blackwood, the same age as my father when he sat in this chair with me on his knee, I look, in the night, out at the back. I have always preferred to sit in the kitchen.

He was, for a time, said to be the best basketmaker on the Levels, not the fastest, but the crown of best was seen by people who knew the preferred crown. Anyone could be fast, leave odd ends and rough borders, but the best basketmaker was seen to beat his work so close you couldn't see daylight. When my father knew he was the best he knew he'd be the next to give up, and though I was a master by then, I became his boy again, until he stopped.

He could make more types of baskets than I can name.

Cockle pads, Fisking maunds, hundreds of Withy Butts, Seedlips, Creels, Winchesters, Swills, Flaskets, Hampers, Panniers, Pottles and Punnets, Wiskets, Fishtraps, Butter flats and Sieves.

When he was fourteen he was apprenticed to Slocombe, a 50-hour week, sorting, soaking and carrying, 4d. an hour. He moved quickly to working on the plank, after two tradesmen took work in Bridgwater. He earned a piece-work rate of 11d. an hour by his seventeenth birthday, making eight baskets a day.

Then he slipped off a ladder and landed badly. He broke his legs and put a rib into one lung. War broke out but he was excused, because from that day on he couldn't walk without a limp. Towards the end of the fighting he was ordered to make parachute panniers by the Ministry of Defence, and forced to work all sorts of imported willow. He never told me much, he was a strong man, and didn't want to be at home while the others were away. He never saw a German aeroplane, and spent months, after it was over, avoiding old friends. I thought it was to do with fighting, but when packets of OMO appeared in wives' windows again, people understood.

He was often with women until he met my mother, and she told him to get out of Slocombe's apron and work in the old wash house, the workshop. She tamed him. Slocombe took that badly. It caused trouble. Slocombe tried to put my mother against my father by telling terrible stories about what he'd fought in the war: the temptations of the flesh, Amy Endicott, Joy Farthing; and he suggested that more than one child born since bore more than a close resemblance to father. Slocombe made one mistake; he faced her as she spoke, and she hit him so hard, with her hand, that he bled from the nose for hours, and dripped all the way home to Kingsbury.

Old Man Out.

The Farthings were the first people to put work his way, once he was on his own; there was a plague of rabbits in

Devon, and he made hundreds of rectangular baskets, 28 ×
18 × 18, with pole holes, for the bunny butchers in London.
It didn't take Slocombe long to come round to the idea that
it was foolish to keep work from a good basketmaker so, to
start with, had him make Winchesters, really a spiteful
thing to do, Winchesters are for bottles and require par-
titions. For their size, they take too long in making, but
Slocombe had that sort of mind.

All the time so many tos and fros between work for other
basketmakers and firms was going on with my father, my
mother built a shed and kept one hundred laying hens in
the field beyond the orchard. She was from an old poultry-
keeping family. She had chickens lay 220 eggs a year, an
average year 20,000 went through her hands to the
egg man. She cleared a space in the store shed, where
she packed them onto pallets. All these eggs saw us
through Januaries and Februaries when neither Slocombe,
Farthing, or anyone, had work for my father.

Something happened when she had me. Dick was the
first child I knew. When I left school I was taken by my
father for apprenticeship. I became his boy, like he had
been Slocombe's, and carried and soaked, doing all the
things boys do, or did; it's finished. Nobody has appren-
tices now, not since the cost of willow was one pound ten in
1970 and eleven pounds nothing within ten years. No one's
that mad. When I was old enough to learn bases and wales,
he had me on stake ups for a year, nothing but bases in the
morning and stake ups the rest of the day.

It was a day like this when my mother went to Langport
to return some milk churns, slung over the handle bars of
her bike. It was a morning in May, like the first day of true
summer. In every direction, the air shimmered over the
ground as if fires were burning, out of sight, in the earth.
That year, whatever year it was, the withies shot like no
year since. On a hot day, even the dampness of the workshop was burnt out, so father checked my mother was well
down the road, churns banging against the sides of her

bicycle, before saying we should leave everything and go for a walk. He was like this. Soft.

'Don't forget the egg man – eleven o'clock,' were her last words as she biked off, but we didn't remember, we jumped the orchard wall, walked past the chickens, and down onto the moor.

In the fields, amongst the purple cuckooflowers and primrose patches, my father's instructive names, the fires from deep in the earth burned on, and the haze rose in walls of solid heat. In leather boots, my feet swelled in their woollen socks, summer wear, so we took them off, tied the laces together and swung them off our shoulders. This was unheard of for men to do; as we walked then I thought, this is the day I am here with my father, and he's saying 'you can see me do this now, you're a man'. We squashed through the moor, across the bridge below Muchelney Abbey, where the river is widening and deep, running towards Langport. We didn't think about the egg man. We didn't bother with the way we were meant to behave.

I took her near this place before they rebuilt the bridge, and we swam in the river, something my father never did, he never went so far. Water was for other things besides swimming in. I thought that, like other things he told me, until she changed my mind. Was I like Dick to her, like Dick was to me? She didn't wear much in the river, even though the road was busy and no trees bank the river for private shelter. The water was dirty, and I never got over the thought of pike racing for my legs with huge mouthfuls of needle-sharp teeth. She didn't care. Eel the size of firemen's hose, she swam across to the bank and back. I went in to show I could, but swam shallowly, and got back to the bank to hold her towel.

'I came here with my father,' I said.

'It's beautiful.'

'He took his boots off.'

'His boots?'

'That was a big thing then. To me. Nobody took them off unless they were going to bed.'

We walked back along the river bank, towards a stand of ash trees, rested our backs against their trunks and smoked cigarettes. I never thought, walking there with my father, that one day I would walk at the same place with her. I never dreamt a girl like that existed. We sat in silence, Muriel, I. She said terrible things like 'life is a sexually-transmitted disease with a 100% mortality rate'. She was full of clever sentences.

A cockerel crowed, a cloud crossed the sun, my father sat up, and shouted '*Eggman!*' The bird called again, an answer came, back and forth through the heat. We were up and running, sweating and puffing through the moor, not noticing river or willow, heading towards the sun, back to Blackwood. My father was in it, no question. The egg man always called on Friday, my mother was going to have a hundred eggs waiting an extra four days.

I didn't like that idea, watching him as we crossed South Moor. He took his watch from a cotton-wool filled tobacco tin to find it was 11:45. A river of sweat poured down my back, another off my forehead, another towards home, and the orchard wall, greying the moor ahead.

'Better get these on,' he said, swinging the boots off his shoulder. We hopped into the orchard, put our hands in our pockets, and walked through the trees with an air of purpose, hoping to look like we'd been somewhere important at short notice, but unsuccessfully. I hung back, he told me to go to the workshop. I couldn't bear the thought of the noise.

'Where you think you've been? What? Just took yourselves off? Fancied a stroll before lunch? You know, you're as much use as someone who's never here. I spend half the time looking after you, the other half on the chickens, what happens the minute I ask you to lift a finger?'

My father's mouth would open. She would say what she always did: don't answer.

'Don't answer!' She'd wind her arm up. Father wouldn't be able to do anything but wait, look at the view, sweat some more and feel the same sweat trickle down his back. I would hear a crash, but instead, a shout.

'Billy!'

I went back outside. Father was there, 'He's only just coming!' And I watched as the egg man drove into the yard.

'Sorry I'm late,' he said, 'the truck broke down at Middlezoy, had to walk miles for the mechanic', and at that moment, with a graceful curve of wheels, chrome, rubber, hair and grease, my mother appeared, a smile on her face, for if anything melted those brass knuckles a bike ride would.

6

May. Swifts. Horse chestnuts, candles of flowers. Fresh lapwings. The sun shone in a clear blue sky, a gentle breeze coasted by, scrubbing the damp from the walls of the house. In the hedge beside the road to Blackwood, like froths on green beer, blackthorn blossomed, and in that lane, someone whistling on a bike rode by. I was sitting outside, on the wall, and nodded hello.

I tilted my head to catch the sun on my face, I could hear my mother in the kitchen with a saucepan, and my father, opening the workshop, going to the tank. Two miles away, Higher Burrow Hill rose from the moor; I had been there many times since the night we were caught in Drove, and I'd stared down at the house, but it had been empty, I hadn't been there again. I was Billy, sixteen, boy now to my father, like a joke.

43

'Where are you?' he shouted, I jumped down off the wall, went to sort bundles, to be his slave.

Since that night, Dick and I had been around, though for months we'd been separated at school and forbidden to visit each other's homes. Because my mother and his were friends – I suppose friends is right – sooner or later we would be about together again.

This day, I did my work, had tea, and went to get Dick.

'I'm off,' I said.

'Don't be late.'

I went to fetch him.

'You coming?' I shouted.

We walked to the canal and across West Moor towards Higher Burrow. We were talking about one of our teachers. There had been a story in the paper about him. Mr Eric Gremner had been up to something. We'd known it all along.

Dick was working for Chedzoy, learning farming, milking by machine, tractor driving, mending gates and fences. He had a packet of cigarettes and a box of matches, we climbed Burrow Hill and sat under the tree, chewing grass, looking down at the orchards around Kingsbury and Lambrook. Amongst the trees, there were many patches of bluebells, like pools of water, we watched a mare and foal rubbing against the trunks, rustling the leaves and young fruit.

'I got him to do anything,' Dick said, 'goes like a bullet. Fetch 'em boy! Bring 'em back, bring 'em back!' He was boasting about a ginger dog at Chedzoy's, Hector, who had taken to him, he claimed, and now saved miles of trudging over the moors.

'Like a bullet. Knows every cow by sight, counts them. He's off looking, if there's one short, two short, ten short. Each one. Saves me miles. Chedzoy hates me for it, always taking about his dog. His dog nothing.' He lit two cigarettes and passed me one.

You could see for miles on a clear day, past places I knew

44

to places I didn't know at all. Where a cloudless sky met the land, miles away, that district was covered in a blue mist, the grazed fields burnt patches of yellow into the view. Closer to the hill, where a single oak or elm stood beside a rhine, or a herd of cows lay in a field, the land was deep green, the houses like single bricks.

'He is, don't know what I'd do without him. Have to walk miles. Then they won't let me take him home, say he'd soon as heel it back to their place. Don't see why.'

He stood up, climbed on the triangulation point, and shouted, 'Let me take him home.' 'Get down,' I said, 'people'll think you're mad.'

'They know I am.'

'True,' I said, and walked to the edge of the hill, from where it gave a view of Drove House, its orchard, outhouses and surroundings. The sun was beginning to sink on that first real summer day, still warm, still a gentle breeze, and scent of tobacco, smoked outdoors. It was odd to see what was happening, and for a moment I stood, hearing, not listening to the far-off sounds, the men's shouts and heaves.

'Dick!' I shouted, 'Quick!'

'What?'

'Look at this!'

'What?'

'This.'

'What?'

'A removal van.'

Someone was moving into Drove House, someone or somebodies, there was a woman, organizing the men who were carrying tea chests and beds. All the windows were open, it looked stranger than when I had looked back that stormy winter night, five years ago. We watched as the men carried some pictures out of their van and into the house.

'Pictures?' said Dick.

'Why not?'

It was hard to organize my mind, all my life Drove House

45

had been empty, people didn't know who it belonged to, nobody in their senses would live there, not if they got to know what I knew. The egg man said a farmer's wife lost her cat up a tree and called him in to get it down. He did it; two minutes later, backing out of her yard, he ran the same cat over, killed it.

I set off down the hill, was walking on my own for a while before Dick came running down and pulled me back.

'Where you going?'

'Get a look. Where you think?'

'All right?'

We reached the bottom, and sat under a hedge at the top of the orchard, and watched, through the trees, three men in dust coats, carrying furniture out of the van, down a ramp and into the house. They carried more pictures than I had ever seen, some massive ones in gilt frames of people on horses with small heads and huge haunches. There came tables and a desk, and a pile of carpets and rugs. When they were carrying a wardrobe, before they took it into the house, one of them said, 'Rest Geoff, it'll knacker us.'

Geoff sat on the wall by the gate, with his mate, the boss, and the youngest of the three.

'What you doing?' said the boss to the youngest.

'Eh?'

'Get the thermos!'

'Oh.'

The woman came to the men, and said, 'Tea break?'

They stood up. 'Yes madam.'

'Jolly good.'

They looked at each other, sat down again. She walked away. At sixteen, sat under a hedge, Dick was in love with a dog, bored. 'He's so scrawny. You wouldn't think he'd run like that. The thing is, Chedzoy never worked him, just chained him in the yard, curbing his natural instincts. When I took him out, he knew what to do, all the calls. I

46

didn't have to teach him anything, it was all there, natural, in his brain.'

'Yes.'

'Are you listening?'

'Course.'

The men carried a cupboard, careful, careful about it, but the one in front, the youngest, stepped off the ramp before the boss was ready, the cupboard overbalanced and slipped from their hands. It bounced on the ground, and even from where we were I heard it crack, and saw the gash in the wood.

'No!' said the boy.

'You bloody little fool. Bloody, bloody fool,' his boss said.

'I didn't . . .'

'No, you didn't, did you?'

'Did you see that?' I said.

'What?'

He was thinking about Hector. I was thinking about a cupboard. I thought, are we growing apart? He wasn't interested in being by this hedge anymore, he wanted to find a herd of cows for his dog.

'I'm bored,' he said, 'I'm going to Kingsbury.'

'What's there?'

'Maybe something, at least.'

I was watching the men, staring at the damaged cupboard, the boss screaming, waving his arms, when the woman appeared.

'Something wrong?' she said.

'Afraid so, madam,' said the boss.

'Oh dear. Do tell.' The woman spoke with a very clear voice, like she was asking someone to pass the tomatoes at a picnic. The boss shoved the boy in the back.

'It was my fault madam, I didn't see the edge of the ramp,' he pointed. 'I stepped back, lost my balance.'

'Afraid we've damaged it,' said the boss. 'That's what he's trying to say.'

The woman stared at the cupboard, and the piece of

splintered wood. She picked it up and handed it to the boy.

'Never mind,' I heard her say. 'Worse things happen at sea,' and she walked back to the front door. 'Keep up the good work.' She had a mane of hair, piled on her head, some strands had come loose, and flew behind her. Her dress, which looked the wrong size and fifty years out of date, blew around as she disappeared into Drove House.

'I'm going,' said Dick.

'Where?'

'Kingsbury?'

'There's nothing there.'

'I can sit on the wall.'

'It's a nice wall.'

'There's other places.'

'So there are,' I said. He got up, let out a long, high whistle, and walked up the hill, kicking at the ground. He was almost out of sight when he called back.

'Hey, Billy! Come here!' I was thinking about getting up, following him. 'What?' I said. He pointed the way we'd come, and when I reached him, looked and saw someone, walking our way.

'Want another?' he said, passed a fag, and sat down.

'Thought you were going.'

'I'm watching.' He was bored. The person came nearer, a girl, brown hair, shirt, trousers. 'Who's that?' 'I don't know.' She walked with a straight back, her head up and a deliberate step. She didn't see us, reached the orchard, wound through the trees, stopped at one and put her hand on its trunk. She rubbed the bark and put her head against it.

'Nutter,' he said.

She went over to the woman organizing the removal men and said something; we were too far away to hear what.

The men finished. They stood with the woman and the girl.

'We should have stayed down there,' I said.

'Why?'

I didn't reply.

The boss shook hands with the woman while the other two loaded some sheets onto the lorry. They closed the ramp, climbed into the cab, and after reversing by the foot in the yard, missing the orchard wall, the lean-to twice, and the front porch, drove off, down the road to Curry Rivel.

It was quiet a moment, as we sat on the hill, and I watched Drove House and beyond; Dick, bored.

'Now what?' he said.

I was very angry, 'How should I know?' I shouted. 'Why'd you want me to tell you what we should do! It's all the time!'

'It isn't.'

'It is. You know it is. Ever since, I don't know . . .'

He got up. 'I'm going to Kingsbury.'

'Go on then.'

'I will.'

He set off up the hill, I walked down and when I looked back he was gone. When I reached the hedge, I walked through the trees myself, until I found one with a long, low branch, screened from the house by a pile of stones, where I could sit, lean back and not be seen. Nothing happened until the woman and the girl came from the house with a tray of tea, to sit in chairs in the garden. The girl put the tray on the lawn and sat down, let out a sigh I could hear, a sigh high and breathy, like a bird. Neither said anything, they looked straight ahead, the air was filled with the sounds of singing insects, cockerels crowing, back and forth, far away, the gentle hum of bees, the noise of tractors in the lanes, and passing cars.

'It's so quiet,' the girl said, suddenly.

'Yes. Strange, at first,' the woman said, 'shall I be mother?'

They drank their tea, it was getting late. They hadn't said much, just tat about the removal men and the damaged cupboard, the woman really didn't mind. I got up to leave, but my legs had gone to sleep and I stumbled; but they weren't talking, I made a noise, and when I glanced up from my hiding place, they were looking at me. As my head appeared, I saw the girl stand up and say, 'There's someone there.'

It was getting late, spring evenings were deceptive, suddenly the light gone, and the warmth. I looked up, and saw clouds blown in, the sky darkened.

I ran up Burrow Hill, and down the other side to the Kingsbury road. It had cooled, I was there in short sleeves, but felt safer on the road with its high hedges, bluebells in the orchards. When I reached the village, I was passing an old garage when I heard a voice call, 'Billy!' I turned to look but there was no one there, just two old ladies by the shop and some kids I didn't know, throwing a ball. 'Billy!' again, 'Over here!' I looked and saw Dick, framed in a door on the other side of the road.

'What's on?' I said.

He laughed. I crossed over, he let me in, pushing me in the back as I went by, and closed the door. It was gloomy, the only light came from a dirty window in the roof, but as my eyes became accustomed, I could see a workbench, old barrels, engines, lumps of broken machinery.

'Who's this?' said another voice, but I was not afraid.

The garage stank of cider. The owner of that voice leant out of the shadows – Mr Jackson who'd worked at Chedzoy's years ago, still went up there, but spent more time in his well-known drink shop.

'It's Billy. My mate,' said Dick.

'Who?'

'I told you, Billy! From Blackwood!'

'Billy from Blackwood,' Jackson said, 'Well! Sit down whoever you are, Billy from Blackwood. Have a drink!' He was drunk and passed me a mug of green cider, strands of undissolvable clear jelly floating in it.

'Thanks,' I said.

'Drink up!'

50

'You ought to open that door,' I said.

'What for?'

'Let some light in.'

'And everybody in the street?'

'Two old ladies and a couple of kids?'

'Appearances aren't everything.'

'What?'

'I said . . .' he tried to say the words but gave up. 'Never mind.'

Dick didn't look very well, held his head between his legs, moaning.

'They saw me,' I said.

'What?'

'They saw me.'

'Who?'

'That woman, and the girl.'

'What girl?'

'You know.'

'Where?' He jumped off the bench, spilt his drink and fell over.

'Come on, Dick.'

'Where?'

'Home.'

'Home? I'm staying.'

'You're coming.'

'Make me.'

'You know I couldn't.'

He pulled himself up. 'Okay,' he said.

Jackson didn't care and mumbled about kids. Dick said he'd see him later, or at the farm, but I led the way, and the fresh air made him sick.

'Better?' I asked as I led him back to his direction. He nodded, but wasn't; he would need to be by the time he got home. Dick's father was not particular.

I left him on the road and walked to Blackwood as the moon rose over a new summer night; when I reached the house I watched my father through the window walking into the front room with a basket of logs. He put them by the fireplace, straightened, and put a hand to his back. I heard my mother in the chicken run. 'You girls,' she shouted, 'you girls will be the death of me.'

7

We drove to Bob Wright's for some willow. The van had never sounded so bad. My father sat on his hands to keep the springs out, pressed his feet against the bulkhead and gave me directions along lanes I'd known since I could walk. When we got behind another, dawdling ahead, he leant over, pressed the horn, jumped up and down, shouted, but they didn't let us pass, even by Muchelney pull-in, they just swerved into the middle of the road without looking.

'Peasants!' he screamed, waving a fist at them. 'Move over!'

'We weren't going any faster before we met them,' I said. 'They're probably doing us a favour.'

'How's that?'

I told him what I thought of the van.

'Heap!' he cried. 'It's older than you.'

'Exactly.'

'You want me to buy something flash that'll be a pile of rust in a couple of years?' I took my hand off the steering wheel, and peeled a flake of metal from the dashboard.

'Like this?' I said.

'Like what?'

'That not rust?'

'Paint bubbling, happens on old cars,' and he tossed it out of the window.

I drove to Langport, then along the main road through Oath Lock, where the lane runs beside the river on one side and the railway line on the other, to Stan Moor. Wright lived in a riverside house with sixteen acres of his own withy beds and ten more rented. He grew Black Maul on all his own land, and five of the rented, but was ripping out five acres of Black Spaniard to replace with New Kind, the best working withy of all time.

'Says who?'

'Slocombe.'

'Ha!'

He was in the stripping shed, whitening.

'That,' he said, pointing at the van, 'deserves a medal.' He took me to one side and said, 'I'll have a word.'

'What about?' said owl ears, springing up and rubbing his hands where the springs had impressed red circles into the skin.

'Sorry?'

'You will be.'

Wright looked cow eyes at my father.

'What you going to have a word with me about? My van?'

'No.'

'Think I'll be needing a new one?'

'Me?'

'Take that look off your face. Find us our stuff.'

'You whitening?' I asked. We always ask people if they're doing something we know they're doing.

A pair of swans flew as far north as Burrowbridge Mump before losing height and landing on a spit of land beneath the walls of a water board house. Bob Wright, a bachelor, led us to his store shed.

'Tea for anyone?' called his mother.

'Tea?' Bob asked.

'Thank you, Mrs Wright. You'd like some, wouldn't you, Billy?'

'Yes.'

She disappeared and the door flapped shut on the shed, my father looked over the willow with an expert eye and congratulated Wright on sheen, straightness, etc, etc.

We carried the bundles and stacked them in the van, before walking up the bank and staring down; the river was low and grey, the shelving mud thick and shiny. The swans took off, three hundred yards up-stream, Mrs Wright came out and called us in for tea.

The front room, where my father sat down and counted bank notes, was dominated by a long, brightly-lit aquarium. Tiny fish darted behind plastic castles and rubber weed, and Mrs Wright, when she'd poured tea, stood beside me and said how much each one cost. They were tropicals and required the water at an exact temperature.

We sat round the table with small cups of tea but huge buns and pastries. My father's hand hesitated over a cherry cake.

'Just tuck in,' said Mrs Wright. 'You boys have been working hard.'

We were full and leaving by the front door when Bob said for us to come out the back door so we could go down through the yard to the pound house.

'I've got some stuff burn holes in your boots.' In one corner of the house stood two barrels of cider, laid in cradles with tiny china cups hanging beneath the taps. He lifted one of them off, tossed its contents on the ground, and poured three mugs.

'That's beautiful,' my old man said, and it was good, deep amber.

'Sure,' said Bob. 'Mind, it'll kick you on the way back.'

'Change from Jackson's,' I said.

'Jackson?' said Bob.

'What you know about him?' my father turned round on me.

'I see him around,' I said, 'met Dick at the garage, the other day, drunk.'

'Who?'

'Both of them.'

'I'm having a word with the boy's father.'

When we drove home, back towards Langport, I turned

back on the main road, just another way home. You drop down into Drayton, and past the church. There's an ancient house with leaded windows, you take a sharp corner, the road straightens to the north of South Moor, and runs towards the old railway, the river and Muchelney. It seemed suddenly very hot in the cab, as the sun streamed in at us. I looked at my father, he had turned off-colour, like the bloom on an unripe sloe. I took one hand off the wheel, I felt unwell myself, and shook him. He went, 'Grrr.'

'Father?'

'Mmm . . . grr.'

I had to stop the van anyway, I was feeling strange, pulled in by the railway embankment, came over hot and cold; I needed fresh air, the hot cab, the smell of chickens and freshly boiled willow. I opened the door and flopped out onto the verge. I lay in the grass for a moment, before pulling myself up and staggering round to the passenger door. I tapped on the window.

'Wake up, hey!'

He looked very ill, more like someone else than a person. I opened the door, and he dropped out of his seat like a sack of potatoes, until he hit his head on the ground and jumped up, shouting, 'Where am I? What's going on?'

'We've stopped for a minute.'

'Stopped? Why? What for? We're not home yet . . .' but then he grabbed his head, wheeled around and was sick. He looked up from this, wiping his mouth, sheet white, mumbled about Wright's cider being a boot of a brew, before staggering off towards the embankment where he slumped down, on the slope, amongst the primroses. I joined him for a minute, until we looked at each other, got back up and walked towards the road. Holding onto the van, we were both sick, I first, he again, while the girl from Drove House cycled by, her hair streaming out in the breeze she made, humming a tune, breaking from the melody only to wish us good afternoon. I couldn't say anything, as a stream of illness was occupying my mouth, but my father was polite enough to say, 'And to you', before spraying the windscreen.

I managed a sideways look, distorted by the angle of my head to her, as she disappeared in the direction we'd come. I saw her two brown legs glistening with sweat beneath a pair of white shorts, and the arch of her back humping at the bike as she pedalled, but felt ill again, and saw no more.

My old man worried, 'Mind this doesn't get any further,' he said. I pumped the windscreen washers.

'You kidding?' I said.

'No.'

'Then what about her?'

'Who's her?'

'The girl on the bike.'

'Foreigner, student. Right here, take the fork, careful on the bend.'

'She's not.'

'Who says?'

'She's living at Drove House.'

'What?'

'Dick and I saw them move in.'

'Them?'

'Dick and I.'

He told me when to take the left to Blackwood, and before we turned into the yard, I slowed down to look in the mirror, smoothed my collar, straightened my hair, but when we pulled up my mother appeared, shouting,

'You took your bloody time.'

I didn't feel too bad.

Tea was a quiet affair, the old man and I picked at our food, while she stared at us shouting 'What's the matter with you?' and other things too obvious to answer. She flustered with her apron at the plates. Then she shouted, 'The chickens'll be grateful', and swept them away. 'Don't suppose your lordships will want the suet pudding?' We shook our heads. She ate enough for three, so none was wasted.

'Get out of my sight. Do something useful,' she screamed. My old man went to the kitchen garden and sat in the tool shed with a geographical magazine. I went to Drove House.

I didn't phone Dick, just set off, not wanting him bored on me, as the sun went down. When I reached Burrow, I walked round the hill and into Drove orchard, and in dimming light sat beneath an apple tree. A downstairs light came on, and I watched the older woman walk into the front room with a box, put it on the table, and leave. I could see half-unpacked tea chests and piles of books, while I shivered at a cold gust of wind that blew through the apples.

A sound rose above the noise of the gathering storm and distant hum of traffic, rhythmic clanking from the lane to the house, before it reached a pitch and the girl came cycling round the corner, to stop at the front door. She swung her leg over the saddle, propped the bike by the porch, and disappeared. I got up, watched her swallowed by the house and crept closer in the dark, so close I could read the spines of some of the books stacked in the lit, but empty front room:

There.
Fortunate to be around: Ruth Baxter's life in pictures.
The pond.
Zen explains baking!
Correct your faults? Don't. Expand on them.

These were some of the titles. I saw a glass-fronted cabinet of dark wood, and a collection of shapes, mainly pieces of stone cleaned and polished, on a chest of drawers. Some pictures stacked against the wall, the top one of the pile, a grey scene of a lake, with rows of breaking waves stretching as far as the eye could see. I had pressed my nose against the window pane, trying to read the words *Collins etymological and reference dictionary*, when the woman came through the door to the room, followed by the girl, carrying cups. They threw some boxes and blankets off a sofa, sat down, and I heard them moan.

I turned away from the window and stood in the yard, watching for a few minutes, as the night drew in. Did they know about the ghosts? They didn't look nervous. I couldn't stand and peep. I decided to leave, went through the orchard and up Burrow Hill. When I reached the tree, I looked back at the house, the single light twinkling in the dark, and stood there until it blinked out, and another light came on upstairs.

The lane to Kingston was a long dark tunnel in the night, the branches of overgrown willow and hazel thrashed in strengthening wind as I walked past the turning to East Lambrook, and rain began to fall. She didn't look like any girl round here. Had she read those books? Should I feel threatened? Should I have studied harder? Was there any point in going near Drove House again?

A line of light streamed from Jackson's garage, and above the sound of wind and rain came the noise of people drinking green cider. Someone had a radio turned up, an argument was brewing. I didn't join them.

8

The wind and rain of the night turned to storm, the sky became a scream of hard, grey clouds; rain lashed against my window as I got out of bed, walked across the landing, and found someone in the bathroom.

'Busy!' shouted my mother. 'Go and let the hens out.' To think it was May; I crossed the yard in boots, the dust of a day before turned to mud, and when I opened them, the chickens just stood in the door of their house, staring out at the rain, like they knew they weren't fish.

By the time I got back to the bathroom, my old man had

taken up residence, I wasn't going to wait half an hour, so went down again, and washed in the kitchen sink, before mother appeared with colanders of eggs.

'Get your face out of my sink! Eggs to wash!' I went outside, and watched as a distant stand of poplar bent in the storm, and young leaves, ripped off before their time, flew in the wind.

'Stormy day,' I said, sitting at the table, breakfast cooking.

'Don't know what you're doing. It isn't ready yet. Your father's not down . . .' The scarf she wore, to keep her hair out of the chickens, was at its best first thing. Neatly tucked in, little rolls of material, a V at the back, pushed underneath a huge bun of hair, she fingered it with a free hand and shouted, 'Make yourself useful. Wash some eggs.'

The postman saved me, as I heard his weary tread, the click of the letter box, and the gentle pufftt as two letters dropped onto the mat.

'I'll get them!' I said.

'You'll not get out of it,' she screamed, but by the time I was back in the kitchen, my father was at his place, eating.

One letter was a postcard from Uncle Ray, my mother's younger brother, the only person who knew how to get her to talk quiet; but he was in Scotland, so of little help.

'It's from Uncle Ray!' she yelled, 'A picture of Scotland!' 'A Brave Piper of The Glens' stood beneath a lake-bound castle, a banner reading 'Greetings from Bonnie Scotland!' printed across the bottom of the picture. She read the card, and said, 'Listen to what he says. "I am staying at Mrs Robert's again, food good as usual though so far four days rain. Went to the castle yesterday but didn't see this chap! Love from Uncle Ray." Isn't that interesting?' she shouted. 'What Uncle Ray says!'

The other letter was a bill from Stan Raymond for the car, when the exhaust fell off. My father stuffed it in his sock.

'Anything?' she screamed.

'No.'

I went to load up for a trip to Exeter, twenty-five log baskets, a dozen trugs and fourteen oblong shoppers, all a week late for Sanderson, Wrigley and Butt, Ironmongers of Force Street. My mother came out to the yard with a saucepan of peeling and crusts, steaming in the rain, for the chickens.

'Is he ready?' I sat in the van, staring at the weather. He came out of the house ten minutes later, slumped in the passenger seat and said, 'I'll drive.'

'You won't,' I said, and before he had a chance to try anything, had it running, and was out of the yard, waving at the old girl stooping over her chickens, as we turned left and into the road.

'Whooo! All right,' he said,

As I drove, towards Ilminster, I was thinking about the old man's ways, learnt from his apprentice years, and how they irritated me. They went round and round in my head, arguments with no end. I always had to leave the inside ends for him to trim, even now, while he'd make that an excuse to go round the basket with a ruler. He sat in the van, sucking his gums. He removed his top plate and began to pick pieces of bacon from between the teeth.

Out of Ilminster, travelling west, the land rises so you can see as far as the eye can see, but not today, nothing but cloud and rain, and as the old man didn't want to talk but just stare out of the window, I was thinking about Dick, and how he was the type to end up picking meat out of his false teeth. Something about his way of walking, down the road to Chedzoy's.

'Want one?' he offered me a cigarette.

'No thanks.'

The wipers couldn't cope; they barely got across the windscreen. I drove with my chin resting on the steering wheel, as rain dripped in through the roof. A lorry overtook us on the stretch outside Honiton, threw up gallons of mud and water, while a car tried to overtake it, and we were pushed towards the verge.

'Bloody maniacs.'

He stared at the wet scenery with a gloomy face, our breath steaming the glass, doodled in the condensation with a finger, smoked another cigarette, and again said 'maniacs'. He'd always thought he'd make something of himself, more than a basketmaker, cut ice, but it was something he'd never had any choice in. He was a boy when the school children in Somerset were given time off to hand-strip willow, he was a baby in the withy beds, sat by a cradle of cider and bread, no choice. He had visions, he claimed, where he saw things and was able to see that same thing somewhere else later, like at the pictures, on the television, or on a walk; he said he wished he could paint. The only picture in the workshop is called 'In the basket-maker's shop Widow Garson found Sammy, with her arms around little Sue's neck, trying to comfort her'. A white-haired man with a beard, sat on a chair, with a basket between his legs, his eyes closed, worked a border, while a dog watched, two small children and the widow in the doorway watched; a crude watercolour, but my father would have painted it cruder. He was never out of the starting blocks, he was never even given a pair of running shoes, in the free country of his youth, he would never do anything but what was coming. I have had better chances but chose this, but only these days, because there is nothing else to do. I was wondering what the girl from Drove House had done to deserve her blessings when there was a crack from the engine, the van jolted, and I was forced to steer into the verge to avoid a coach.

'What happened!' the old man jumped in his seat. 'Why we stopped?' He'd been asleep.

'Something went. I thought you had it fixed.'

'The exhaust . . .'

'It was in the engine.'

'You sure?'

'Fan belt?'

'No.'

He didn't know the first thing. We watched the rain fall, the traffic thundered past.

'I suppose I've got to,' I said.

'Well done. You'll have it fixed.'

Ten minutes later, and a new belt, I climbed back into my seat, soaked, lucky to be alive, so I could listen to him crow.

'Lucky I kept a fresh one in the van,' he said.

'You thought it was something else, you wouldn't have a clue.'

'Who thought of carrying a spare?'

'It got left by mistake when they fixed the exhaust.'

'Good, isn't it?'

'What?'

'The new exhaust. Quieter. A good run, like this, do it the world of good.'

Of the three, Sanderson Wrigley and Butt, the last Wrigley had died in 1947, nobody knew where Mr Sanderson was, and Mr Butt was definitely out for sandwiches. I was met by a sub-manager, a small man with the habit of picking flesh off the edge of his thumb with an index finger. Tiny pieces of dry, white skin dropped to the floor, as I told him we were outside with the baskets.

'About time,' he said, rudely. 'They were meant to be here last week. What's been going on?'

'You didn't get a phone call?'

'No.'

'Then someone's let you down . . .' I paused to read the name on the plastic tag pinned to his chest, 'Mr Podmore.'

'Oh?'

'Someone here,' I said. He looked doubtful.

'My father phoned to say we were waiting for white sevens.'

'White sevens?'

'Seven foot, white.'

'Seven foot, white?'

'It's willow.'

'And?'

'So we were held up, nothing to do with us. We can't tell what's available all the time. Not our fault.'

I gave him our invoice, he told me to stack the order in the back. I went out to the van, we unloaded the baskets, and left them with a surly boy who said, 'Thanks a lot.'

'If he says anything,' I said, 'about a phone call, just say you did.' Mr Podmore tried to give us a cheque, but the old man insisted on cash; no reason, he was in one of those moods. The journey had upset him.

'I've no cash here.'

'Then get some.'

'I can't. Not till Mr Butt comes back from his sandwiches.'

'Sandwiches?'

'He always gets them. Calls it his little foible, the boss doing the office boy's job.'

'We'll wait.'

'He'll be half an hour.'

'We'll be back in half an hour,' my father said, and with an arthritic wave left the office, calling me over his shoulder, 'Come on Billy, we'll get a pint.'

An hour later, in the van, a wad of notes, still warm from Mr Butt's hand, tucked close to my father's chest, we were travelling in a dangerous manner along Exmouth Road, towards the motorway. With five pints of cider down his neck my father was driving.

'I can drive on an M5!' he shouted, though he never had before. We didn't need to go that way, but there lay the challenge, and as we drove down the sliproad, and the traffic increased, my old man took on a determined expression and headed for the lane carrying the least number of vehicles. We hadn't got two hundred yards before a car came up behind us so fast it had to swerve to avoid a collision, the driver flashing his lights and waving a fist. I was not going to say much to my father, but did manage, 'You're in the wrong lane.'

'They're all going the same direction, I can drive down any lane I like.'

63

'But.'

'Shut up.'

A coach bore down, flashing and hooting, swerving into the middle lane, the passengers leaning over in their seats, expressions of fear and alarm on their faces. My father watched a kestrel, hovering over the verge, the sun broke through scattering cloud.

'Motorways give you time to really look around,' he said. 'All you have to do is point in the right direction.' He turned and smiled at me, 'We'll come this way every time.'

'This is the fast lane.'

'Yes,' he said.

'I mean,' I said, 'there are three lanes to each carriage-way.'

'What?'

'Pull over,' I shouted, pointing.

'But they're going slowly.'

'So are we.'

Another car.

'Please,' I pleaded, in the end, pulling at the steering wheel.

'All right, all right,' he said, but hadn't finished, he didn't look over his shoulder or in the mirror, it was hard down with the left hand and across two lanes of traffic. Lucky to be alive, again, but the old man sucked his teeth, asked me to light a cigarette, and got lost outside Bridgwater.

We didn't get home till seven, the egg man was at Blackwood, and as we climbed out of the van, heads dull, my mother screamed, 'Where the bloody hell have you been?'

The egg man, whose name was, I think, Brian, but I'd heard him called Steve, was carrying a bucket from the store.

'Len's had to help me,' she pointed at the egg man.

'We got lost,' said my father.

'Well done.'

'Outside Bridgwater.'

'Bridgwater? Doing what in Bridgwater?'

'Not in, outside.'

'Outside!'

'He missed the turn on the motorway,' I said.

'What were you doing on a motorway?'

'Trying to get home.'

'Trying to get home?'

It continued, my mother repeating everything my father said, only as a question; the egg man stood in the doorway of the store shed with a bucket in his hand, while I corrected errors of fact. The sun set in a blaze of diagonals, shafts of red and orange light burning long stripes into the darkening sky above the shed and the egg man's head. An owl called from an oak tree, single flowers closed for the night in the rustling hedgerows. Sober people in fast cars drove into the night to get pissed. Children slept. The two women at Drove House sat in their front room surrounded by broken cardboard boxes full of kitchen utensils.

Next day, my father came to the workshop first thing, to help me sort. He was moving bundles of willow to a spot where I didn't want them. I had sat down, and was working, when he said, 'Beautiful day.' It was. The storm had cleared, leaving stacked blue skies, the odd fleck of cloud brushing the west, but the wind had veered south, a wood pigeon flapped by, and in the distance, the clack-clack of Chedzoy's machines clacked off, the sun rose high in the sky; that was how it was.

Dick got a motorbike, so I could hear him coming for miles, given a calm day, like a paralytic bee. Life changed, a new love in his life; I didn't care, he took me pillion down an old drove, it was all right, but I never had his passion, I drove a van.

Disco time. Friday night. Burrowbridge Hall, ten miles away beyond Stan Moor and the Glastonbury road. I stood in the yard while Dick revved his motorbike.

'Coming?' He wasn't asking. My old man appeared round the corner from the orchard, whistling 'The Sun Shines Bright On My Old Kentucky Home', a dead racoon slung over his shoulder.

'All right, boys?' he said. 'Nothing like it.'

My mother sailed from the back door with a bucket of potato peelings, yelling, 'Where the hell have you been?'

'You coming, you listening even?' Dick said, slipping into his crash helmet.

'I suppose so, I don't know.'

'I'll pick you up.'

'On that?'

He gave it some throttle. My mother looked, came over, 'You put my hens off laying,' she screamed, 'and I'll have that motorcycle.'

'Sure,' he said. I shrugged, I didn't care, the time had long gone when I was responsible for the ideas we had; brawn had ousted brains, not that we really ever had either.

I was cleaning my teeth when my father shouted Dick was waiting.

'Why?'

'I'll ask.'

'You coming?' He was in the house, shouting up the stairs, 'Why you cleaning your teeth?'

'Don't know.'

'Come on. Get some clothes on.' I hadn't thought since the last time it was mentioned. I hadn't thought about anything except whether a greengrocer in Taunton would mind his baskets late. A few days before I'd gone for a walk towards Martock, and seen lapwings in huge flocks. I hadn't remembered it was Friday night and my presence expected on the back of his motorbike.

'I'll bring the van,' I said.

'Father's using it.' Screamed.

'Am I?' came a small voice from the front room.

'Hurdles from Chedzoy!'

'Oh.'

The men were forgetting things in the house.

'You're coming with me to the disco?' He spelt the words. I resigned myself to going, spat toothpaste, washed, and dried with slow, deliberate and relaxed actions.

'All right,' I said, 'just sit on the wall for five minutes.' I displayed five fingers.

'Mind you don't,' my mother shouted.

I sat on the bed and stared at the view of South Moor and the valley of The Isle. The Isle is a leak of a river, but a ribbon of clear blue in the dying day. A pair of swans flew in the gentle evening wind, their long necks bobbing in rhythm with their wings; pfftt, pfftt, pfftt. I tied my bootlaces, to meet my chauffeur.

Dick's style of motorcycling was interesting; I got this idea that I was going to fall off. He raced down to the bridge, took the right to Stathe, the bend at Wick, past the houses, throwing old ladies back from their doorsteps, dogs from the middle of the road, and opened the throttle to take the long stretch to Oath Lock. I shouted 'There's no hurry', but he turned round in his seat, swerved in the road and said 'I know'. He asked if I wanted to get there any faster. What I said made no difference. We flew the railway bridge and the straight between the tracks and the river, he accelerated past a pair of cars on the road through Stathe, and I felt the taste of apricots come up. My mouth was dry, I saw a water rat in the river, swimming from our bank to the other. A crow, startled by the noise, exploded out of an orchard tree. It was night when we came to the crossroads at Burrowbridge.

The Disco car park was filling with many different cars of similar styles, Cortinas and Escorts with badly riveted flared wheel arches. It was never me. I left Dick to find his mates, and went into the hall for no reason at all. Things were warming up; some Greasers were throwing beer at girls who liked this. Loud music was coming from speakers on the stage as an arrangement of coloured lights played patterns over the walls. People sat in ranked steel and canvas stackable chairs, the crowd by the bar hatch grew, a blue haze of tobacco smoke floated in the air, like a heavenly floor all around us.

Dick slapped me on the back, 'Enjoy yourself,' he said. 'There you go.' He put a glass in my hand and took a gulp from his, like he was eating it. His eyes looked wild, his untidy hair its blackest, another gulp, punch to the arm, 'Got to go!' and a wink, he was off, back to his friends. I watched him urge one to drink a pint in one, then he did the same with the rest of his, pushed through the crowd and ordered more.

Two girls stood up and danced together, the greasers watched with quick, shy glances, looked at their glasses, drank some more. The girls moved awkwardly in their clothes and shoes, like lame flamingos in clogs or badly-fitting slippers. I didn't see anyone I wanted, so took my drink into the night and stood for a minute with my back to the river, the sky filled with a thousand stars. I heard a few more cars arrive, a motorbike, an owl call, the thump thump thump disco beat sound, and the odd yelp of dancers.

'Finished that yet?' Dick staggered out, two pints drunk, shirt unbuttoned to the waist to display three curly black hairs around his navel.

'Drink up,' he slobbered, 'We've serious . . .' and put an arm out to steady himself on my shoulder.

'Dick?' I said.

'Your round.'

'You're drunk.'

'I know, you my grandmother?' He spilt some beer on my boot. 'Sorry.' He went back to the hall. I propped myself against the door to watch the moon rise, as a car pulled up, the driver got out, and in the shadows, I could see her, the girl from Drove House. She stopped in passing, stood by the door, and looked at me, for a second, in the half-light, like she knew me from somewhere neither of us had visited.

'Hello.'

'Hello,' she said, and walked into the hall. I followed her to the bar, leant over the crush and tapped her on the shoulder.

'Buy you a drink?'

'No thanks.'

It had taken a little courage to get in there, but the refusal was expected. In the lights of the disco, a band of freckles pulsed across her nose. She waved the barman a note, and shouted over the heads of three other people. She carried her glass to a bench by the door.

'I can afford it.'

'What?'

'To buy you a drink.'

She drank, looked around the hall.

'I've seen you somewhere,' she said.

'Have you?'

'We haven't been here long.'

'We?'

'My mum, me.'

'No?'

69

'We came from London.'

'London?'

'You ever been?'

'No.'

'Like to?'

'Wouldn't mind.'

'And what about you?' she said.

'What about me?'

'Where do you live?'

'Blackwood.'

'Round here?'

'Near Kingsbury.'

'Episcopi?'

'Yes.'

'That's near us! Drove House.'

'Yes, I . . .' I stopped myself.

'You know it? Under the hill with the tree.'

'Higher Burrow Hill.'

'You do!'

'A little,' I said, now I had given myself away.

'Maybe,' she said, 'you were the one we saw in the orchard when we moved in.'

'No. I was working that day.'

'What day?'

'The day you moved . . .' I murdered myself.

'So it was . . .'

'I . . .' I got up, 'You want another?'

We stood in the car park while a fight developed by the lamp post. She'd come to the disco as she'd driven back late from Bridgwater and passed by, she'd wandered into it by chance, just fancying a drink.

'I could show you around,' I said.

She laughed again. 'Around where?'

'I don't know; the Moor, Kingsbury, Taunton?'

'Much to show?'

'Depends.'

'I'll see. I've got to go.'

70

'Now?'

'I was late before I arrived.'

We walked to her car.

'What's your name?'

'Billy.'

'I'm Muriel.'

'Call.'

'I will.'

I had to find Dick. I looked round the back, I looked round the front, I looked in the toilets and behind all the cars and motorbikes, I looked in the room behind the stage. He wasn't there. He wasn't at the bar. He wasn't dancing. He couldn't. He wasn't standing by the door. He wasn't with his mates. I looked behind some dustbins. I walked one hundred yards one way along the river bank, and another hundred yards up the bank the other way. He wasn't there. He wasn't in a car. I walked along the road for a while, but couldn't find him. I looked in the hedge and under the wall round the car park. I looked back in the hall. I asked a few people if they'd seen him. Someone thought he was behind the stage. I looked; he wasn't. I sat down on a canvas chair while last orders were called. A few people drifted away, but the disco carried on. I went out and looked round the bank, again, along the bank, calling 'Dick! Dick!' I thought he'd fallen in the river, drunk, sluiced down the steep, muddy bank into the torrent. By the light of the stars and a vague moon, I scanned the water, hopelessly; a plastic carrier bag, stuck to the mud on the opposite bank, caught my eye. I looked upstream towards the bridge, and saw somebody, leaning over the side, dropping stones into the water. A car drew up and the person climbed in. I walked back towards the hall, looked the other side of the car park wall, but he wasn't there. People were revving motorbikes, his was where he'd left it. I looked back in the hall. I didn't want to walk ten miles home, and was looking for a lift when he appeared, around the back, with a slip and a large bottle.

'Where the hell have you been?'

'Down Dan's.' He pointed along the bank towards a house, its downstairs lights glowing in the night. 'Saw you with a girl, I wasn't hanging about!' He sat on the ground and said, 'Urgh!'

'Come on,' I said, 'you're my horse.'

'What?'

'Motorbike, remember: brum-brums?' I did some throttling with my wrist.

'Oh yeah,' he said, and fell back on the grass, spilling his bottle and stretching his arms above his head. He did not look capable. I went back to the hall, and filled a bucket with water, carried it back to where he was lying, but he'd gone. I found him by the dustbins, so I said, 'Dick!' and when he looked up, threw the water at him.

'Whaa!' he groaned.

'Wake up!' I shouted.

The journey back to Blackwood is not a comfortable experience to remember. Some events from my life appeared in motion in front of my eyes, playing themselves out on the back of Dick's crash helmet. I remembered my father telling a bald man the price of petrol was enough to make your hair stand on end. I remember seeing a police car in Langport, and stopping to wheel the bike behind a hedge in Huish. I heard a voice cry, 'What bloody time do you think this is?' but my own voice said, 'Dick brought me home.'

10

'Kink the league!'
  'Both sides?'
  'Put your thumb on the spot, where you kink it.'
  'It'll split.'

'It will. It doesn't matter; let's see.'

'It's holding.'

'Then pull the ends together. Like this. Tie them; then work the stakes like usual.'

I hate basketmaking. We are working. My old man told me the mystery tour story. He was a boy, taken to stay with his mother's sister, Aunt Janet, in Sheffield, where the snow turns black and Chinese people eat their tea in the rain. One day, he'd been taken by Donald, his uncle, a large man with a steel leg, on a mystery tour. The Hodges Coach Co. offered the trip; leaving at ten, back by nine. On the journey, Donald drank from a bottle he carried in a red duffle leg, unscrewed his leg and put it in the luggage rack. He fell asleep outside Bristol.

When he awoke, the party was disembarking at its Mystery Tour destination, the interesting country market town of Taunton. They had five hours to spend on their own, so caught a bus to Kingsbury, had a cup of tea with his grandparents, and then my father and Great Uncle Donald went back to Sheffield. I've heard it a thousand times.

The sun was shining, another warm day. My father sat in the corner and sorted sticks. I was making shopping baskets, fitting them with split hazel stakes.

'When Uncle Donald took his leg off, my mother fainted. He was someone the family could have done without. He was hauling cattle north. Aunt Janet met him at Taunton Market, she disappeared, people thought he'd stolen her.'

My father had met my mother before her parents died and Blackwood came to her, but he'd only lived in Kingsbury, so couldn't steal her anywhere. She came, shouting, 'Where you put my buckets?'

'What?'

'My buckets!'

In five strides she crossed the yard from the house to the workshop door, barring all the light from the place as she stood, framed in the valley of The Isle. One of the jobs I'd inherited from my father was the cleaning of six galvanized buckets every day.

'Have you washed them?' she screamed, 'bet you haven't.'

I hadn't. I got up and went to wash the buckets.

I was round the back of the workshop by the taps, when I heard a clanking. It stopped. Footsteps. The egg man? I was on the third bucket, scrubbing it round with a brush when I heard a row break out in the yard. Mother was shouting at the egg man again, he hated Blackwood. I stacked the buckets, carried them around the side of the shed where Muriel stood next to her bike, opening her mouth to shout: 'I only came to say hello to Billy. You always scream your head off at innocent people? Does he live here? I met him at the disco. You know?' My mother hung her chin off her face like a banana, stared up and down at Muriel, while I appeared with the buckets.

'Hello!' I said to Muriel, ignoring my mother. 'I never thought you'd come.'

'I said I would.' She had yellow ribbons plaited into her hair, a blue vest, shorts, again.

'My buckets?'

'I remember,' I said.

'If I'm not interrupting anything.'

'Bike only just make it,' she said, holding it away from her body and giving it a mean look.

'I heard it!'

'Clean, are they?'

'What a beautiful day. Are they always like this?' she said.

'Seems like it, at the moment.'

'If I may!' My mother grabbed the buckets, and stalked back to the house.

'Your mum?'

'Sorry. She shouts a lot.' I scratched my leg. I wasn't sure what to do with my hands.

'My mother never shouts.'

74

'Never?'

'Sometimes wish she would.'

'Sometimes wish mine'd shut up.' I pointed. Muriel laughed, threw her head back. 'Stick the bike against the wall,' I said.

'You work here?'

'Yes.'

'Growing willow?'

'Making baskets.'

'Great! Show me.' I didn't think it was great, but I'd show her where I did it.

'Here.'

I pushed the workshop door open. We walked into the gloom. My father tried to get up.

'Morning!' he said, to her. 'Who are you?' She gave a little jump.

'My father,' I said.

'Muriel.'

'Muriel? A friend of Billy's?'

'Yes.'

'It's a lovely name.'

'Oh?'

'Oh yes,' he said.

'You . . .' she laughed, he struggled to get off the floor, but clenched the small of his back and slumped down again.

'Arthritis,' he said. 'I'd get up but can't.'

'I'll give you a hand,' she said, and before he could say no, had her arms under his shoulders and heaved him up.

'My dear, thank you!'

Muriel was a forward, modern girl, and though I was modern in the sense that I lived now, I could have lived fifty years ago and not noticed the difference. She had a huge, wide smile, and showed it to my father, who couldn't believe his luck.

'Call me Jack,' he said, and stuck his hand out.

'Okay, Jack.'

Okay, Jack?

'Elevenses?' he said to me.

'Yes; you want some tea?'

'Great.'

'We'll be on the bank; thanks Billy,' he said, and by a surprised arm, took Muriel from the workshop, round the back and onto the river bank. He'd charm honey from the bees.

'What you doing?' mother shouted, as I made the drinks.

'Want a cup?'

'Course I do, only one who's worked for it.' She threw a sock at me.

While the kettle boiled, I stood under the porch and watched Muriel wave her arms at the old man. He laughed. The sun shone, the kettle boiled, and I carried three cups outside. My mother was banging upstairs, with sheets, I left hers on the draining board, to cool.

As I climbed the bank, Muriel was saying, 'So when they found her, she was stuck with her foot down a rabbit hole! She'd shouted "Help!" for hours, she said. Any excuse for a bit of attention.'

'Tea?' I said, bending to pass a cup first to Muriel, then to him.

'Thank you.'

We drank.

'Urgh!' said Muriel. 'Sugar!'

'Sorry?'

'You put sugar in it?'

'Yes.'

'Didn't you bother to ask if she took it?' I didn't say anything. I went and made another cup.

He came down the bank as I climbed back up, 'Nice girl,' he said, 'she's waiting for that.'

Chedzoy's cows had worked their way across the field opposite, their smell drifted over the water to us.

'Been doing anything?' I said.

'We went to Exeter yesterday, shopping. Mum bought

me a new dress; she got a hat. Straw one, plenty of plastic fruit.'

'Oh.'

'We're going to Taunton this afternoon.'

'Nice.'

'Suppose you go there all the time.'

'Sometimes. Saturday, market.'

She followed me to the workshop.

'Are you going to show me around?' She was a straightforward girl, asking me out.

'You want to?'

'I wouldn't ask if I didn't.'

'No.'

'You're so funny,' she said.

'Funny?'

'No. Not funny ha-ha, just funny; I don't know.' She looked into my eyes. 'You've lovely eyes,' she said. I didn't know what to say; nobody said things like that.

'Really,' she said.

'Oh.'

'Oh what.'

'Nothing.'

She got up and stood by the door, watching my mother walk across the yard.

'Thanks,' I said. She looked at me. The light caught her face.

'You're welcome,' she said. 'Your orchard?' She pointed.

'Want to see?'

'Great!'

'I built a tree house in the orchard at your place.'

'Drove House?'

'When I was a kid, with Dick.'

'Dick?'

'My mate. Sort of.'

'Sort of?'

'Spends all his time on his bike now, getting drunk.'

'And what about you?'

77

'What about me?'

I showed her the apple trees, pointed out three Fox-whelps and the Kingsbury Blacks. I explained they don't require blending to produce good cider.

'Taking the day off?' my mother shouted from behind the chicken house. Muriel looked at her watch.

'I should be home,' she said.

'So when shall I show you around?'

'Anytime, pick me up, I'll give you the number.'

'Who's that?' my mother shouted, as Muriel disappeared down the road. I told her. I didn't want a scene. I was working in the shed when the old man came back, and sat in the corner.

'You're a dark horse,' he said. 'Never knew you had it in you.'

'Might have done,' I said.

'Nice girl,' he said, 'not from round here.'

'You saw her before, on the bike, down Muchelney Embankment.'

'I haven't got a bike.'

'She has.'

'Did it make a noise?'

'We were coming back from Wright's, his cider had us.'

'Who?'

'Us.'

'No, her.'

'Muriel.'

'So where's she living?'

'Drove House. With her mother.'

'Drove House,' he said, quietly, and flicked a piece of willow between his thumb and finger.

'I told you then,' I said, 'when we were sick.'

I liked it that she came out with what she was thinking. She wore ribbon in her hair. She walked towards things so the things she was walking towards knew she was coming. She moved her head when she talked, brushing strands of

78

hair away from her eyes with a casual movement of small, brown hands.

When we were eating tea, my mother asked about Muriel, but the old man told her to stop going on. He ate rice pudding and sat at table with a cigarette.

On my own, that evening, I took a walk over Thorney Moor to Muchelney and stood in the churchyard to watch the sun sink. A gardener was working in front of the priest's house, and carried his fork round the back. I heard the whine of Dick's motorbike, coming up the road from Longport, and crouched behind a gravestone until it was gone. A bowl of wilted daffodils sat beside me; 'Gone To Sleep.' Nobody came to church, nobody tended any of the graves. An aeroplane roared down towards me, a long, low descent, hanging in the air, waiting to land at Yeovilton. The sun sank when I wasn't looking, behind a bank of thin cloud, but the sky turned red, the gentle heat of the day went 'snap' and was gone.

11

I didn't wait to call Muriel; on the way home, I stopped at the phone box. Her mother answered, they'd just got back from Taunton, where she'd bought a thing for doing spaghetti.

'Can I speak to Muriel?'

'Of course, how nice, hold the line.'

There was a pause, I listened to feet disappear up the hall. *'Muriel! M-U-R-I-E-L! Telephone!'* 'Coming!'

'Hello?'

'Hello,' I said.

'Who's that?'

'Billy.'

'Billy?'

79

'This afternoon?'

'Oh, Billy!' she interrupted, 'that was quick.'

'Quick?'

'I didn't expect you'd phone today. We're only just back from Taunton.'

'Your mother said.'

'She bought a thing for making spaghetti.'

'Lucky for some.'

'Yeah!' she said.

'I was phoning . . .' why?

'Yes?'

'To find out when you wanted me to show, well, go really, around?'

'Show me the sights?'

'What? It's a terrible line.'

'The sights! You're going to show me the sights?'

'If you want.'

'I wouldn't have asked if I didn't want.'

'No, I suppose . . .'

'You get a day off?'

'Wednesday.'

'Wednesday, hang on. What time?'

'Any time.'

'Ten? Eleven?'

'Ten?'

'Eleven?'

'Okay.'

'I'll pick you up.'

'You know the way?'

'Ten?'

'Wednesday,' she said.

'*Muriel!*' I heard her mother say, 'be a love and help a tick.'

'I'm on the phone,' she shouted, and then to me, 'duty calls.'

'Eh?'

'Got to run. Mum wants me.'

'Don't they always?' I said, quite smart, I thought. She laughed.

'Wednesday?' she said.

'Okay.'

'See you then.'

'Bye,' I said.

'Bye,' and she put the phone down. I stood in a pond of cigarette ends and small strips of paper torn from the directory, with the receiver in my hand, looking at the night. There was a knock on the door, peering in at me stood a very small, old lady.

'You finished?' she said.

Wednesday's weather gave early promise, the sun glared off the river and the dew in the fields; calm, a clear, clear blue sky. I left my father in the workshop. He said, 'Glad to have the place to myself.'

I didn't always bother with the day off, and hung around, or went to Langport; taking the van for the day with a basket of sandwiches and beer for two was new. My mother made the picnic, 'There's no point taking a girl out if you don't make sure she'll be comfortable.' She handed me the basket with a gentle look in her eyes; she'd just got into the habit of shouting.

'Drive carefully,' she said. She reached in her apron pocket and pulled out a faded stalk of lavender. 'Pick her some flowers,' she said. I mixed anemones from the garden with some honeysuckle from the hedge.

That sun, I can still feel it. When I pulled up to the front door, Muriel's mother came out, smiled, walked over.

'Hello,' she said. 'I'm Anne.' She offered me her hand, I took it. She was wearing a paint-stained apron and said, 'Just dabbling.' She had dark blue eyes, set deep in her face, and wore a scarf, like my mother, just done a different way. Long locks of grey hair hung out of it, and brushed her face as she walked me to the house.

81

'Muriel's talked about you,' she said – I felt myself blush – adding, 'Nothing terrible' – noticing. She was alert, quick on her feet. Her daughter appeared in the doorway before we reached the step.

'Good morning!'

'Hello Muriel.'

She was wearing a pink cotton dress and a white shirt, and picked a canvas bag off the hallway table.

"Got any grub?' she asked.

'Yes.'

'Me too!' she said. 'All sorts. You drink lager?'

'Yes.'

'Cheese and ham sandwiches, apple pies, bananas?'

I nodded. Anne stood between us, and laid her arm across Muriel's shoulder, a smile creased her face. A tiny group of yellow paint spots clustered together on her chin, like a phantom beard.

'Are they for me?' Muriel pointed at the flowers.

'Oh,' I said, 'I forgot. Yes.'

'Let me,' her mother said, 'I'll put them in water. You two, off now, and don't get back till late.'

'Where to?' Muriel asked, threw her bag into the back of the van and eased herself into the passenger seat spring position. We drove west, out of the valley of The Isle, through the lanes to Curry Mallet.

'This is knackered,' she said, 'we could've taken the mini.'

'Who's showing you these sights?'

'You are.'

'My sights, my van.' Something else I thought, then, smart, pointing to things along the way.

I know a hill, on the county border, where a line of trees climbs its spine and the locals burn fires. The weather, I knew it would, collapsed at midday, the wind strengthened, and a bank of grey cloud blew up from the west. Spots appeared on the windscreen. The wipers hadn't been fixed. As the rain increased, and what Muriel talked about turned into what I talked about, we met a herd of cows walking from one Blackdown field to another. I slowed to a crawl, with my hands on the top of the steering wheel and my chin on my hands, staring at the farmer's dog, chasing back and forth across the road, and I thought, a little, about Dick and Hector. It would be raining in Kingsbury, he'd be fretting over his bike getting wet, and the dog, who was beginning to take a back seat, would be laid flat under a lean-to, with a look in his eyes. 'Cows. Let's get them! Sod the bike.'

Muriel's voice echoed around the van, the empty plastic sacks, an old basket, the small piles of straw, like a tune, whistled, when you don't know you're whistling. Steam rose off the cows, hot, damp, bugged, as they turned off the road into one of the fields overlooking the odd, wooded clefts of land that drop to Hemyock, and Honiton.

She leant across and tweaked my cheek. I felt her thumb and finger, warm against my skin, and she said, 'You're so . . . nice and . . . and, oh! I don't know, there! You know? Picked!'

I didn't, and thought she wasn't very good at explaining herself, then neither was I, how could I talk? But she had had education, not like mine, though I had been interested, she had been brought up to know things to do with words, and to do with being able to act, as a girl, more like a man than most men do. Open. Strong and direct. She knew what she wanted.

'This rain!' she said, 'Does it always rain like this?'

'No,' I said.

'And aren't we a long way from home?'

'Yes, but there's a hill I want to show you, perfect for a picnic. Maybe we'll have to go somewhere else now.'

'Why?' she said, like it was a natural thing to sit in the rain. 'Bit of rain never hurt anyone.'

'Don't be so sure,' I said.

'Chicken.' She said it. I'd sit on the hill if I froze to death, to show her. City girl didn't know what it was like at three hundred feet. I had looked on a map. I knew. Exposed to wind from every direction, huddled beneath a scorched scar the locals had made.

I parked in the track above Bottom Farm, and we walked the quarter mile to the summit in drizzle, the first sign of cleaner weather behind us.

'That's amazing!' she said, when we'd put our stuff on the ground, and with my hands in my pockets, and her dress, damp, pressed against the backs of her thighs, sat down.

She'd brought ham and cheese sandwiches the size of stamps, cut by her mother on a marble slab. Her mother painted pictures in watercolour of earth and sky. Muriel said they were monuments to nature, alive with the truth of their subject. I didn't know what she meant, but said I'd look at them. We sat, facing east, as the grey clouds were blown away, down, like a curtain in front of us. The sun at our backs, propped on a blanket, I offered her a cigarette.

'Thanks.'

We ate the picnic as the weather cleared, and the distant hills revealed themselves. North, the Brendons, climbing to Exmoor; the Quantocks, the Blackdowns in the south, and the villages and towns strung out towards Taunton. I grew hot, and the moisture, in the grass, in heating, released a sweet smell.

I made her follow my finger as I pointed out the border, following the course of a river, weaving along a hedge, through gates and farms. I did not bore her. For a moment, she laid her hand on my arm, to stop me as I talked, and asked about something I was pointing at.

'What's that?'

'What?'

'Where you're pointing.'

'The farm?'

'Up against the barn.'

'The machine?'

'Yes.'

'I don't know.' She smiled.

'It's hotter than ever.' She reached up and pulled off her jumper, tossed it behind her head and lay back. 'Hotter,' she said, and ran a hand over her forehead, while I stared at a herd of red cows, rubies in the grass, chewing the cud below us. A gull flew by, rooks, the ground softened and full of worms grazed the fields.

Muriel fell asleep, and I watched her in this, her body hardly moving, a whisper of hair blowing gently across her face. Her eyes quivered, and she made a small sound. I sipped some beer. I lit another cigarette. She said something in her sleep, but I couldn't hear. Then she became restless, but that was all.

I finished the sandwiches, stood up, and left her, to walk to the crest of the hill and down the other side. In a sheltered corner of the field, growing from a banked hedge, primroses, in fat, yellow clumps. I collected enough to fill my fist, wandering along, spilling red earth out of the bank as I picked. Where the wind and rain had washed the place, the roots of hazels and elders had been exposed to the sun, and bleached white, like bones.

I carried the flowers back to where she lay, still asleep, I put them by her face, she twitched her nose, and brought up a hand to brush them away.

'Ah,' she went. 'Mmm.'

'Hello?'

'Billy!'

'I picked them for you.'

'Primroses. Billy. Flowers and more flowers.'

'You like them?'

'Of course.'

'You fell asleep. I picked them down there,' I pointed.

'You should have woken me.'

'You looked so peaceful.'

'So you left me to the mercies of the, the . . .' She spread her arms.

'Sheep?' I said.

'Sheep?'

'Mauled by a sheep. It happens all the time.'

I drove, Muriel relaxed, the van was hot, the drive home too short. I have memories, stored for future comfort, and these stand up to the best. Wheeling birds, golden leaves, a butterfly, warming itself on the bonnet. What a beautiful day. She rolled me a cigarette. I could scent her tobacco; we met a wagon of hay, the driver waved us past, and gave me a wink, like he was Cupid.

12

A thing to make my mother mad, hot weather. It was a hot week.

'Weather for it!' my father said, his arm around my mother's waist, his head resting in her armpit.

'Aagh!' she let out, pushed him away, went to the store, the galvanized lid banged back and the chickens started. The egg man was ill, a different one got lost at Long Load. My mother had fifty pallets stacked under sacking in the workshop. She moved them in without a word; I didn't mind. I was piling willow in the shed when Dick turned up. Chedzoy had given him a job: go to Langport and buy three buckets. Chedzoy had made a joke. He said Dick could wear the buckets on his head on the way home. Dick rode into the yard with three buckets on his head.

'Aaagh!' yelled my mother, as he slewed to a halt beside me.

'Hey!' he said, 'I've come from Langport like this!' Taking the bend at Huish, the buckets had slipped down the helmet to cover his eyes, but he hadn't cared, and rode into

86

a wall. His front mudguard was tied to the seat with a piece of string.

'You're a bloody mistake,' I said.

'Thanks.'

'Hey!' my mother shouted, he swivelled round, 'Yes, you!' She disliked the sight of Dick. She didn't like his motorbike putting the chickens off.

'And you!' she pointed at me. We didn't like this, and for once, united in approach.

'You . . .' she took Dick by the collar, 'won't ride your bike on the property like that.'

'No.'

'Because if you do, riding a motorbike will become, for you, painful, in the future.'

'Yes.'

'And you!' she grabbed me by an ear, 'never use that language near me again.'

'Language?' She was a bloody hypocrite.

'You know, don't play with me. I heard.' As we walked away, she hit Dick on top of his crash helmet.

'Oi!' she shouted, 'remember!'

'She's mad,' he whispered, picking up his buckets.

'I know.'

He sat by the workshop window. 'What's this then?' he said.

'What?'

'I saw you!'

'When?'

'Wednesday? Thursday? Last week, the day it rained. Wednesday.'

'So?'

'I saw you!'

'Where?'

'Isle Brewers, come on,' he said, 'you know what.' He winked.

'So what?'

'She's from Drove House. I went up there too.'

87

'What?' I shouted, 'what you doing there?'

'It's a free country. I can go where I like. Took Hector out.'

'Oh yes?'

'Yeah, he hadn't been out for a day. All right?'

I didn't like the idea of his nose in it, now I knew someone he didn't, and had done something I didn't want to tell him about. Needn't either.

'Come on,' he said, 'everyone knows about it!' Which they didn't.

'Look!' I pointed a finger. 'It's nothing to do with you.'

'Oh!' he yelled, 'aren't we the one.'

'Oi!' came a voice, my father, 'where's the scrap?'

'He's going on,' I said, pointing at Dick.

'I only asked where he went.'

'Minute ago you knew.'

'We've all been doing that,' my father said. 'Didn't get any sense out of him. Got a girl though. Pretty.'

'Shut it,' I said.

'Ha!' went Dick.

'And to you.'

'Start again and I'll fetch mother,' said the old man, 'you're a couple of kids.'

'He might be . . .' I said.

'Enough of that,' said Dick, 'I know what's going on.'

'I hope not,' said the old man.

'What's going on?' screamed my mother, looking over my father's head, a silence falling upon the workshop, as the temperature climbed and the air filled with pollen. To be in the cool grass on Higher Burrow with a girl like Muriel; with Muriel. I wanted to argue with her, not with all these same people. The crop of swallows flew around the yard, singing at the insects.

'Nothing,' I said.

'Sounds like a lot of it,' she shouted.

I stood, 'He,' I yelled, 'is getting up my nose.' I pointed at

Dick. My parents blocked the door. I wanted to leave. I shouted 'Excuse me!'

I climbed the bank behind the workshop and sat by the river. A mad poet, Coleridge, said the river Parret looked as filthy as if the 'Parrots' of the House of Commons had been washing their consciences therein. I said this to old man Chedzoy when I was ten, on the way home from school where I'd learnt it, and he'd said, 'Bugger off.' In the heat, I lay on my back, closed my eyes and listened to Dick wonder where I was.

My mother shouted, 'Sulking up the bank?'

'Mooning after his bit of stuff!' yelled Dick. 'I'm off. I've had enough.' He had buckets to deliver, I could lay on the bank all afternoon, if I wanted. I was my own man and didn't have to be anywhere. Goodbye, Dick.

I liked Muriel. She had grown irregular teeth framed in moist, marshy lips. However quickly I pictured her in my mind, it would not be soon enough before my mother screamed, 'You lying on that bank all day? Slocombe's not waiting all week.' I was glad Dick had gone. But when I got up and looked down at the yard, he hadn't. One bucket had fallen off his head, and he'd run it over. My father was talking.

'Hear the one,' he said, 'about the fireman and the cat?' We had. 'Old woman's cat got stuck up a tree, so she called the fire brigade. They turn up, climb the tree, rescue the cat. Old woman says, "Oh thank you so much! Do come inside and have a cup of tea."'

Dick was trying to squeeze the bucket back into shape. 'He'll kill me,' he was saying, 'no!' He looked worried. It was hot. The bucket was split in one place and bent in three.

'Tell you what,' I said.

'What?'

'He's going to kill you.'

'After tea, they were backing the fire engine down the drive and ran the cat over. Killed it. Just like that bucket.' The old man pointed. 'You'll never get it fixed.'

'He's going to kill me.'
'More than likely.'
'Ha!' I laughed.
'Laugh?' shouted Dick.
'You!' screamed my mother.
'Thank you,' said my father.

13

At Thorney Mills there is a silted old pool where teal and eel swim, sheltered by the old building. A cast iron wheel hangs on the wall beneath its eaves; the river Parret, a drain of a river, is a better place than any to catch eels. Like the poet Coleridge, we learnt about eels at school. Nobody knows why they travel over 3000 miles from a sea of weed in the Atlantic Ocean, after breeding with American cousins, to arrive in the Parret at Thorney's silted pool. There are many ways to cook and many ways to catch eel. Smoked, they are delicious, boiled, poached, baked? Nets, traps, line, rayballing? The river was thick, clotting, perfect weather, two days of sunshine turned muggy, then a series of thunderstorms. Rayballing weather. Eels, four or five years old, swimming in the pool. Their adult eyes, though not fully grown, and their long golden bodies, swivelling through the dark water, feeding before their stomachs wither and they swim, swollen with fat, away and against the currents to the weedy sea again, where they were born, to birth their eggs. In nine months they will be dead, far away. Cunning fish, to live so long and travel so far to somewhere so small without anyone knowing how.

'Hello?'
'Billy?'
'Yes.'
'I was wondering when you'd call. Happy?'

'Yes.'

'Going to ask me out again?'

'When?'

'Take me fishing. You know how?'

'Rayballing?' I said.

'Pardon?'

'Don't you know what rayballing is?'

'No. You going to tell me?'

'I'll show you.'

We went rayballing one Saturday. The eels never knew we were coming. They swam in their pool, I took a tin bath off the workshop roof, and spent the morning digging.

'You dig any more of them and there'll be none left,' my mother shouted. 'Worm's good for it, the gardener's friend, you know?'

'You want eel pie?' That shut her up.

When I had twenty worms, that was enough, little piles of earth round the garden, I put them in a honey barrel. The eels waited. Some of them were so old they had been rayballed before, and escaped; no other method of fishing reduces the odds so much. No daylight penetrated the pool. An eel could not see its own tail. It smelt for other fish, cruised at them with a fleshy purpose. I walked to Drove House. The van had been misfiring. I didn't blame it. I walked through the orchard, Muriel's mother was sat painting.

'Morning!' I said. She jumped, and made an odd noise.

'Hello Billy, making me jump!' she said.

'Sorry,' I looked at the painting. The canvas was covered with thin lines of green and brown paint beneath a big washy block of blue.

'The light's so good,' she said. I looked at it, it didn't seem different from any other. 'Do you paint?' she asked. I didn't. 'Oh it frees me! Out in the open, give me a paint box, clean canvas, my dear, a morning like this, I'm in my seventh– Listen.' She cocked an ear. 'I wish I could capture it, in paint.' What? I didn't know what she was on about.

91

'What are you two doing today?' she said, wiping the brushes on her smock.

'I'm taking Muriel rayballing.'

'What's that?'

'Ah!' I tapped my nose. 'That'd be telling.'

'You!' she said, and punched my arm gently.

'Morning!' cried Muriel, coming out of the house. 'Mum's painting. Good?'

'Very good.'

'You're just saying that.'

'I know.' I didn't understand pictures, but said they were good. I was just confused.

'You walked?' asked Muriel.

'Yes.'

'Fantastic.'

Her mother turned to me, 'She's got something to show you.'

'You bet.'

We walked round the side of the house, she took my hand, past the lean-to, and parked in the yard was an old ambulance. It looked as if it had been driven off a battlefield. It was the first ambulance I'd seen that could have been called a danger to health. The indicator lights were missing, and where the blue light had flashed, tangled wires hung down. The words 'Ambulance' and 'Health Authority' had been painted over in a shade of paint slightly lighter than the rest. Inside a few metal rods and rolls of wire lay scattered about where ill people had once been laid. It smelt of toilets.

'And goes like a bomb!'

'Does it?' I said, 'where?'

'Anywhere you like.'

'She's so proud of it,' her mother said, poking her head round the front. 'I said, "You find yourself something to give you that little bit of independence." Isn't she clever?'

I nodded.

'I'll get my things,' said Muriel, and disappeared.

'Do you mind?' I asked her mother, crawling underneath.

'Be my guest, make yourself at home,' I stared up at the rotten chassis and the way the steering joints were cracked. The sump was leaking. The silencer was pitted with hundreds of tiny little holes. A birds nest of loose wires had been jammed into a cavity behind the gearbox supports. I was sorting them out when a voice called 'What are you doing?' and *bang*! I sat up and smashed my head on the exhaust pipe. Pieces of rust flaked off and embedded themselves in my skull.

I said 'Yeesh!' at the ambulance.

'No need to be like that.'

'I banged my nut!'

'Why?'

'You surprised me!'

'I surprised you and that made you lie underneath my ambulance? You're crazy.'

'No,' I said, standing, rubbing my head, waiting for her to say 'My poor baby', 'You didn't make me go under there, you surprised me after.'

'After what?'

'After I'd got underneath.'

'Oh.' Pause. 'But why?'

'Why what?'

'Why were you underneath it?'

'I was looking.'

'What for?'

'Something I didn't find.'

Leaping in the driver's seat with a 'Let's go!' and an optimistic wave at her mother, who waved in an equally optimistic way at me, we lurched out of the yard and into the quiet lanes of Somerset. Flocks of startled birds exploded out of trees and hedges as we thundered by, startled cows miscarried, sheep were driven insane with worry. From my position, high above the road, distant farms could be seen, and chickens, running for cover.

93

'Where we going?' she said, 'Fishing? Where's the tackle? You forgot, didn't you? Typical.' She took her hand off the wheel and pinched my cheek. 'Typical man. Mum said, soon as you'd got me alone you'd forget everything like a typical man. I said no, he's different, something about him that's not like everyone else. I've got this feeling, and besides, he's handsome.'

Ha!

'Blackwood,' I said, 'then Thorney Mill pond.' We careered round a bend and the door beside me slid open. I watched the road come up to meet me, then we took a bend the other way, and the door closed, rapping the side of my face for having its head outside.

'Urgh!'

'Is my darling hurt again?'

'Grr.'

'What's rayballing?'

'What?'

'Sorry; I only asked.' She threw the ambulance into a swerve and drove into our yard, in a cloud of dust, inches from my mother's face. I waited.

'Any more of your bloody friends put my hens off,' she screamed, 'and I'll hold you personally responsible.'

'Personally responsible?'

'Don't fancy me!' We picked up the tackle.

The worms escaped the honey barrel on the way to Thorney pool. They were suffering travel sickness. Some of them were ill on the seats, another went into a coma on the floor. In a disused ambulance there was nothing I could do. It died in my hand, its body quivering gently as it went on, a look of peace passing over its face.

'One of the worms has died,' I said.

'I'll dig another for you! Make my day. What did you do today, Muriel? Oh, nothing much, went rayballing, dug a worm.'

Bob Wright has drying fences around the pool, and as a stack of dark cloud gathered in the west, was spreading withies along the wires. I unloaded the bath, and was tying the worms when he said, 'Rayballing today?'

'Reckon on it?'

'Good enough weather,' he said.

But it wasn't. It started to rain. It came as I was floating the bath onto the pool, and Muriel was asking, 'What are you doing?' It rained hard, and with the wind, cold. Bob sat in his van, Muriel sheltered in the Mill. I refused to stop rayballing, but when the worms went wild in the rain, and slipped the knot, I got what I could of them back in the barrel, closed the lid, and got out of the rain myself.

'Muriel!' I cried through the deserted halls, 'Where are you?'

'Here! Find me! If you can!' Bellies of rain blew through smashed windows and open doors, rusted on their hinges. Broken machinery and mouldering bales of material, the gloom and smells of people dead who'd risked fingers and eyes at their work. The wind rattled some old looms.

'Coo-ee!'

'Muriel?'

I climbed open stairs to a loft and its loading doors, slid open to the weather. Broken glass and cardboard boxes lay strewn about the floor, but the view, over the moor, east, from this height, was beautiful. Out of the wind, it was almost sheltered by the open doors, seized pullies hanging over them, to a four storey drop.

'Gotya!' she shouted, and poked me, from behind, in the ribs.

'Don't do that!' I yelled, reeling back and falling on the floor. 'Give me a heart attack!'

'So I'd be here,' she said, 'to give you mouth-to-mouth resuscitation.'

'Oh yes?'

'Yes.'

She crouched down and pulled my body against hers. Tiny rivers of rain ran off her hair and dripped on her face. Kissing she had her eyes closed, I kept mine open, and

95

watched her eyeballs moving beneath their lids, and the end of her nose tucked in by mine. I counted the freckles across her face, she moved her lips, and reached over my shoulders for my arms. She lifted them, with her eyes still closed, and put them round to where I could feel her back. She squeezed hard, so I did the same to her. I closed my eyes, as she let her body fall back, and I was pulled so the top half of my body was lying on her. She rubbed one of her legs against me, I opened my eyes, and she was looking. She had green eyes. They were glazed, and at the edges, watery in the fold of skin. I thought I'd squeeze again, she stopped kissing, and smiled at me. Where her bottom teeth met were tiny stains. She took an arm away and stroked my face with a finger, crooked, running down the skin beneath my cheekbone. She had done this before.

'Done this before?' she said.

'Course' I said, 'I've done everything.'

'Yes?'

'Why not?'

'Oh,' she said, 'never mind,' and grabbed again, and kissed me. She pulled at my jacket, we rolled over so she was on top, and for a moment, sat up, with her legs astride me, and stretched. Beyond her, through the doors, the weather. She put her hands to the back of her neck, flicked her hair and closed her eyes.

'What is it about it?' she said. I didn't know. 'Grr,' she went, and kissed me again. I didn't feel cold. I reached an arm around and touched her face. One side of her head fitted inside my hand. When I curled a finger over the top of her ear and stroked, she moaned.

A car door slammed, I looked up, it had stopped raining. Bob was at his fences again. Muriel got up.

'Come on, lover,' she said.

'Anything.'

As soon as we got out, Bob dived into his van because it started raining again. We sat in the ambulance, I looked at the tin bath, floating on the pond. It was filling with water, not eels. The worms had managed to overbalance the honey barrel, force the lid, and escape. Bob said he wasn't hanging around any longer, banged on the window my side and said, 'See your father next week.'

Muriel and I held hands and stared. The rain lashed against the ambulance and rocked it gently.

I said, 'You've had lots of boyfriends.'

'Have I?'

'I don't know.'

'One thing's certain.'

'What?'

'None of them took me rayballing.'

'But I didn't.'

'You tried.'

The ambulance behaved as we drove home, she took my hand and held it under hers, on the steering wheel. I could feel the engine straining through its pistons, up the steering column, and into the steering wheel itself. The rain muffled the exhaust, and the noise of the loose panels banging and rattling against each other. We didn't say much.

'Me?' I said. She nodded. We were talking very quietly. 'I don't know. I haven't had . . .'

'What?'

'What?'

'You haven't had what?'

'I don't know.' She laughed.

'I do,' she said. I blushed. 'I love that blush,' she said.

'You coming in?' I said, parked on the verge outside Blackwood.

'Should I?'

'If you want.' She sat with me and took my hand. 'Have some tea?' It rained.

'I think . . . I'll go straight home. Have some with mum. Tell her about my day.' She winked.

'You wouldn't.'

'She wouldn't mind.'

'I might.'

'Why? Nothing wrong with two people off rayballing in the pouring rain. Everyone does. We do it all the time.' She laughed at me. I looked hurt. 'I'm sorry,' she said. She put her arms around my neck and kissed me once, quickly, on the lips. I knew what to do.

I stood in the rain beside the ambulance and she said to me, 'What is rayballing?'

'Something close to what we did instead, only with eels.'

14

As my father walked down the market hall, he met Chedzoy. They were talking, someone else walked by carrying ten trays of eggs, my father stepped back and knocked them on the floor. I was outside. A man was trying to sell me a dodgy jacket.

'You want it, go on, try it, yeah, there you go, see?' I didn't. 'Go on. I can see you're a man of taste, look at it, sits on the shoulders perfect, ask anyone. Madam? Over here a moment please. Yes, see this? Does it, or does it not fit like a glove? What? To you my son, at the rock bottom, bottom of the rock price of forty nine pounds. My final offer. Couldn't go lower to save my life.'

I always stare at something in situations where I'm not going to be told what to do. I looked at the eye, neatly sown into the corner of the awning on the next stall. A length of rope held the canvas to its frame, and this strained against the eye in the gusting wind. Saturday. Taunton Market. Somerset were playing at home. The river bridge was crowded with people watching for free over the back of the new pavilion, though most were there for the fatstock. Light, medium and heavy heifers were all making a good price, some lights reaching 88.2p per kg. Simmental bulls were fetching poor money though, around £110, what you'd normally expect to pay for a Friesian. Twenty-nine barren cows averaged 64.3p per kg. I heard a commotion in the hall, and watched as my old man was thrown out of a side door.

'Look,' I said, 'I don't want it, do not want it.' I spelt the words for him, and handed the jacket back. 'You think it fits?' I said to the woman. 'You buy it.'

'It wasn't me it fitted,' she said.

'Doesn't matter. It never fitted me. You two always work together?'

'What you on about?' the bloke said, at the moment my father appeared.

'Got to go,' I said, and to the old man, 'What happened to you?'

'Someone said I owed them a hundred quid.'

'What for?'

'Some eggs.'

'You didn't?'

'Exactly.'

Light lambs made from 146 to 183, av. 157.2 per kg., heavy lambs 128 to 147, av. 134.6. Chedzoy sold a Friesian heifer for £450, the highest price paid all day.

The van hadn't had any work done on it. On the way home, it stalled outside Langport, so two policemen came up and tapped my father on the shoulder as he looked at the distributor.

'Trouble sir?'

'No problem,' he said, sanding the points with the side of a matchbox, 'happens all the time. Only thing that does, mind, this bus's been going since you were fresh out of nappies.' The policeman looked at my father, then at his colleague, who paced around the van, poked the tyres with a boot, bent down at the back and shook his head.

'Have you seen this?' he said.

'What?'

'If you wouldn't mind?'

The old man got sent out when he showed my mother the ticket.

'You bloody fool!' she screamed. 'You don't even need to go to market, it costs you money! Every week!' She slammed a saucepan on the draining board, 'That's the last time, the very last.'

It was a beautiful day. I ached when I thought about Muriel. I let my parents fight it out in the yard, walked down to the orchard, past the chickens, and sat by the river. Their voices carried in the breeze, 'You do this,' and 'I'll do that.' A flock of lapwings moved through a dock patch, their white chests dipping in and out of the leaves. One darted from cover to peck at something in the grass, another followed, another. The sun beat down, some bees in the orchard hedge rhymed with the raised voices from the yard, a door slammed, the bees played alone. I heard my father crunch across to the workshop, shut the door. The river flowed away from the sea with the tide, a bulge of water cruising up the ocean from Argentina, tiring out near Blackwood, pulled by the moon, lived in by eel. A wood pigeon landed in an apple tree. My mother stormed down and shouted, 'You want your message?'

'My message?'

'The girl told you to call!'

'Muriel?'

'That's her name.'

'Why?'

'How should I know?'

Thorney Mill. I could feel her turn me over, her soft hands pinning me down, lowering her face to mine. I felt the rain on my back as I stood by the ambulance and she said she wouldn't come in. It was warm rain, trickling down the inside of my shirt and over my eyes. I licked a drop off my lips and she said 'You'll have to wait.' She smoothed the sleeve of her dress against her skin.

I walked across the fields to see her, with a stick of hazel I'd found in a hedge. I crossed the Isle at the bridge on

South Moor, through dazzling light, slashing at some nettles by a rhine. I saw Anne painting on the slope of Burrow Hill; the view towards Langport and the hills far away. She had turned the house into dots of grey paint surrounded by blobs of green, brown and blue that was not at all like the sky.

'That's not the colour of the sky,' I said.

'It's not the sky.'

'What is it?'

'A picture,' she said.

I thought she'd heard this somewhere, the way it came out of her mouth, like a gun going off or a back, snapping.

'It's what you make it; what's it say to you?'

'Is it a talking picture?' I said.

I could see Muriel in the orchard. She was lying on her front with her legs bent up behind, her dress fallen into the angle they made, reading. She had kicked one shoe off, it lay in the grass beneath her feet, the other dangled on the end of her toes, hesitated, and dropped off. She squinted at us, but the sun was in her eyes, she shaded them with a hand, and waved. I waved back. 'You go on,' her mother said. 'Got to finish, it's strong today.'

A book called *Let's arrange things*, an empty bottle of lager and a plate of crumbs lay beside me on the grass. Muriel was throwing tiny apples from behind a tree. Insects buzzed over the June Drop, a thousand tiny apples shed from their branches by natural selection. I flipped them away with my hands.

'Hey! Beautiful!' she cried.

'What?'

'Catch!' She ran off towards the house, in the front door, and as I caught up, disappeared upstairs. It was cool inside, with pictures on the walls; a field of wildflowers with purple mountains, and some fishermen, stood in a row along a pier. I heard her footsteps above me; a photograph of a Chinese boat, with a huge, ripped sail made from mattresses. A family crouched beneath a canvas covered hoop of cane, it was raining on the Chinese, a boy was stood in the weather, his hand on the rudder, steering downstream. Some other people were standing on the bank, holding fruits, waiting for the boat to tie up. These people were smiling, and behind them, in a hedge of evergreen trees, a troupe of monkeys was eating bananas. One of them was hanging by its tail from a branch. Muriel's head appeared.

'You coming up?' She reached down to me. She looked beautiful. Her dress was white with blue stripes at the hem, neck and sleeves, tied by a cord of silk, printed with pictures of moths. The sun streamed in the window behind her, lighting the ends of her untidy hair. I took her hand as she led me into her mother's room, through the door I'd stood behind and my mother had opened and into her room, with a view over the lean-to, towards the pound house and the Blackdown Hills.

'My room!' she said, and spread her arms. I looked at the bed and blushed. I couldn't help it. 'Blusher!' she said.

'I know; I can't help it . . . I . . .'

'You don't have to,' she said. I didn't know what she meant. 'I know,' she said, 'you're lovely.'

There were photographs on her wall of a man, smoking a cigarette by a fence, and another, playing the violin. She sat on a cushion by the window. We talked about how I'd been bothered by a dodgy bloke selling jackets and she told me about a friend of hers who sold toothpicks and scraps of newspaper embedded in amber. He was someone for whom direction was meaningless and art pure paradox. I told her my father had knocked a lot of eggs onto the floor.

'How'd he do it?'

I said, 'He needed to walk down the aisle.'

We sat together. I didn't know she wore glasses to read. She picked up a magazine and tossed it onto the bed.

'I'm going to London.' She wound a pair of socks around her head and threw them at a chest of drawers.

'When?'

'Day after tomorrow.'

She'd be sat in a room with the traffic roaring beneath, with a bloke saying, 'Art,' pouring amber onto a scrap of paper printed with the words AFTER THE STRIKE WAS HALTED BY, 'is pure paradox'. I couldn't compete, looked at Muriel, but she was gazing out of the window; I didn't think of anything smart to say. The more I thought, the worse it got.

'You mind?' she said.

'Do I?'

'Don't you?'

'Yes,' I said, 'I mind.' The beautiful weather never seemed so dull.

'You jealous?' she asked, throwing a shoe at the door.

'Jealous?'

'You are?'

'Me? What of? Can't be jealous of something when I don't know what it is.'

'You don't know any of my friends.'

'You don't know any of mine.'

'No,' she said, 'but mine . . .' She stopped what she was saying. Her mother had packed her paints away and was walking down the hill towards us. As the sun dipped, the shadows raced, and it grew chill, she walked across the yard and in the door. I listened to her moving around downstairs and the sound of cups being rinsed and laid out.

'Yours?'

'Nothing,' she said.

I felt jealous. She was talking about them being different, but stretched across the floor to where I sat and took my hand. I looked into her eyes and watched the reflection of the sun move across them like a bug. She crooked the little finger of her other hand, ran it down the ridge of my nose, and squeezed. I leant towards her, she closed her eyes to let me kiss her lips. I felt her hand squeeze mine, she shifted her legs. Her mother called up the stairs to ask if I took sugar. I jumped, but Muriel said she didn't mind. I couldn't relax.

'Relax,' she said. I couldn't.

'I can't.'

'Don't worry,' she said, 'change the subject. You tell me something.' I was when Anne walked in.

'Two teas, no sugar both; biscuit?' she said, bending down with a plate. 'Feel free, plenty more in the cupboard.'

'Thanks.'

'I see your father's famous!' she said, passing a newspaper.

HUNT FOR RACOONKNAPPER CALLED OFF.

The hunt for a missing racoon was called off today after a local basketmaker found its body in the river Parret. A spokesman for the Ridgeway Safari Park said the animal escaped last Thursday and had probably been living off the land.

Muriel said she didn't think it had been buying take-aways. Nor did I. I wouldn't tell you about the tea. It tasted of antiperspirant, but I drank it, and imagined Muriel knew what it was.

'Kiss me again,' she said. Her dress slipped off her shoulder and hung over her arm. While we kissed I didn't think about London, but did when we'd finished, stood up, and looked at the dusk from her window. If she could kiss me and ask me to kiss her, she'd be with him, pouting, getting him to put his pan of boiling amber to one side, his moulds and toothpicks, saying 'kiss me'.

As my mother ladled a pile of damp cabbage onto my plate, she told my father that if he picked he'd get no pie. He picked, staring at his shoes, put by the back door.

'Taunton Monday,' he said, 'all done?'

'I spent the whole morning on them. You know I did. Why'd you always ask questions you know the answer to? Why don't you shut up when there's nothing interesting to say?' I was upset. I'd been on my own all day, with my thoughts, in the workshop. I didn't care though, it wasn't my problem that Muriel had gone.

We went to Taunton. The old man sat in the van while I carried two dozen log baskets through the back door of a gardening shop, sneering at a queue of people waiting for a bus. He gave me a tenner, so when we got home, I sat in the van until he got out, then drove to Jackson's garage.

'Dick there?' I whispered.

'Dick?'

'Who wants to know?'

'Billy. You letting me in?' The door opened enough, and Dick shouted, 'The wanderer returns!' I didn't know what any of the people I knew were saying anymore.

'Left you?' he said. 'Gone off with an old fancy man?'

'You don't know anything about it.'

'That's what you think!' He poured some cider. 'Forget her,' he said. 'Better off with a tart you know.' He smelt of rancid butter and in the gloom, picked at the dim outline of the line of fuzz on his top lip. The drink was bitter and did not satisfy my thirst. I sat on a bench listening to him talk about Hector.

'Got told off, told him, I said "You chase cows like that and he'll have you", but Hector, got a mind of his own, the boss gave him a thrashing, thought he'd killed him.'

I said, 'I saw a dog stung to death by hornets.'

'I'm telling you, he won't be doing that again in a hurry.' I said it was six hornets, six killed a sheep dog. Took three hours to die and two vets, writhed round the yard howling and howling, in the evening. They put him in a barn, but the howls echoed into the night like they were solid, like you could go out, grip one with your hand, cut a piece off. Chilling sound. Hornets got armour plating, built like tanks. Look like bombs. You can see their mouths moving, clicking back. They have slanty eyes set back on their heads. Though they have a deadly sting they use it reluctantly, so that dog must have really pissed them off.

I caught a length of jelly on my lips, no light filtered into that place. I felt the juice in my brain, and saw Muriel's lips embedded in amber, pouting at me as they flew by. I touched my knees with my head. Tiny explosions went off all around me, the garage door opened and shut, names called out across a space of darkness, and an odd thump thump on some stairs.

I felt softness all around, and a dampness beside me, a woman shouting and the sound of a motorbike. Eight sad horsemen rode by, small women carrying pancakes left them in the fridge. I was comfortable in bed, I remember.

15

At Thorney Mills there is an old silted pool, where teal and eel swim; rayballing weather again, but I couldn't go, I was working on laundry baskets for the domestic market. It was perfect, another clotting river, high, fast clouds, but it was gloomy in the workshop, an atmosphere heavy with loss. One of mother's finest was laid up in a cardboard box under the window, on no account was I to touch her or make any surprising noises. She had coccidiosis; stood for a day on her own in the run, sick and drawn before the move, and was being treated to a water fast for twenty-four hours. A laxative diet of barley and husks to follow with a clove of garlic for ten days. No other hen would go near her. If she didn't recover, a hatchet would come between her and continued enjoyment of the orchard.

My mother shook her head, and didn't know why she bothered. 'Coccy's deadly; look at this,' she said, handing me a nugget of blood-stained chicken shit. 'Kills the girls for no reason and all that science doesn't make any difference. Might as well know how to cure coccy.' She stroked the

hen's head with her nails, and tucked some straw around
its body.

'Don't you worry about eggs,' she said. 'Just eat up, do
you good.' She nudged some food at the bird but it closed
an eye with a ghastly cloudy lid, and blinked open only
slowly. It opened its beak but nothing happened.

'You watch her,' she said to me, 'and don't shout at your
work.'

There are many diseases of poultry that lead chickens to
the cardboard box. Toe-pecking and pantothematic acid
deficiency in young chicks, to egg-bind and plain boredom
in laying birds. Many treatments are available. My father
brought some tea, and while we drank, stood outside in the
yard watching some teal, packed together like sardines,
flying down to the river behind us. There are many things a
teal enjoys, wading in mud, worms, but nothing more than
the company of its own species. We have eaten them but
they're small and carry little meat. I would prefer a mallard
from Taunton bus station, where they stroll out of the river
around people, and are well fed on many fattening foods. I
would put one of them in a sack anytime, still warm,
plump.

'See them?' he pointed as they flew to the pools.
'Scrawny buggers not worth a toss.'

I sat down. Plastics have taken the domestic laundry
basket market and given it a boxing lesson, but there are
still some people who prefer the sort of thing that ladders
nylons and tears silk shifts to ribbon. Ribbon in her hair,
scarf around her waist, stockings on her legs, a thousand
freckles on her face, one hundred eyes turn to look, see
Muriel, on a street where I could never live. We'd watched a
television programme with the prize of a car, the woman
hadn't won. She got £800 with the champagne 'Pick-a-
trick!' bonus prize, but looked fed up with the idea, and
backed away when a smarming host tried to kiss her cheek.
He'd bumped his chin on her shoulder, while the celebrity
'Femme de Cherie' stood behind them, holding an

envelope. The old man said it was a laugh, but I didn't care, I only saw the street outside the television studio, where men and women drove by on their way to Muriel's.

I spent the afternoon making handles. The egg man arrived and stacked the pallets in his van, checking the invoice and making a joke about putting blown eggs in with the real ones. He had never learned not to crack it.

'Find a blown egg and it'll not be me who's responsible,' she shouted. The egg man was a bit thick. I never spoke to him about it. He lived in ignorance.

Around tea time the ailing chicken died of its own, spared the bloody steel. I took it to the house and put it on the kitchen table.

'Take the thing away!' she screamed. 'I don't want it!' She didn't care once they were dead, and a bird with coccy wasn't edible. 'Dig a hole for it,' she said, 'and burn the box.'

I dug a small grave in the orchard. I warmed my hands over the fire, watching the sun sink into a bank of streaky grey cloud, stood over the cardboard box until it was all gone. I could stand over anything until it was all gone. I stood next to my old man while he planted a row of peas.

'I wanted to stuff that racoon,' he said. 'Don't get the chance often enough.'

'Stuff it?'

'Why not?'

'You ask them?'

'They wouldn't listen. It went for a post mortem; I could have saved them the trouble.'

He straddled the row with his feet, walking backwards, scattering the peas on the ground. His back was hunched. He stopped, put a hand to it, stood up.

'It had a lovely face, beautiful eyes, tiny dog's nose. I've always wanted to stuff an animal. Nothing to it.'

'I'll catch you a rabbit.' He lifted his hat and scratched his head.

'Always wanted to,' he said. 'Would you?'

'If you want.'

'It'll have to be live.'

'All right,' I said, 'I'll use a broody box. Tie the bait to a sprung flap, rabbit picks the bait up, shuts the door. Piece of string. Easy.'

'Borax,' he said.

'What?'

'Borax. I'll need some.'

'Borax?'

'And sulphuric acid, ammonia.'

'You sure?'

'Sure. I read it. Borax, sulphuric acid, ammonia, some salt. Sharp knives, and an eye for the natural pose.' He took another handful of peas. 'An eye for the natural pose,' he said, moving down the row. 'More than just important, it makes or breaks the whole effect, the pose.' I had to find a rabbit willing. He had to avoid my mother. He would need a place to work. Could he get borax? Sulphuric acid? Are they dangerous chemicals? Can you drink them? Could I hear Dick ride by? My father raked some soil over his peas, the teal flew back the way they'd come. One of them laid a turd on his hat.

Muriel came back. She parked her ambulance in the yard and had brought me a present, but wouldn't give it until we were on our own. It was great to see her. She was more beautiful, and talked to my father about how he'd manage on the underground.

'Got to finish these peas,' he said to her, though he had. He was just being nice.

Muriel and I walked along the bank and watched the sun set from the bridge over the Isle. The river Isle, which rises near the village of Dowlish Wake, to the south east of Ilminster, in Somerset. There are seven bridges over the river, which flows for about fourteen miles before joining the Parret near Blackwood. Isle Abbotts and Isle Brewers are its main villages. During the middle of the nineteenth century, the Parret Navigation Company built locks at Thorney, and cut a canal to connect Westport, near Drove House, to the Parret by way of the river Isle. You might think, 'so what', but the man who built the Westport canal was the same Walter Bagehot who became advisor to Disraeli when that man was interested in the Suez Canal.

We walked along the bank to the first bridge from Blackwood, sat in its shade and held hands. The history of canal building in Somerset is an interesting one. We could see the spot on the river where the Westport canal cuts in. It was romantic. She gave me a Dinky Toy ambulance, in a torn box, and I kissed her.

'It's very rare,' she said. 'Collectors pay tops for them.' It was her ambulance. 'I saw it and said "That's it!" You like?'

'I was expecting a toothpick, in a lump of plastic.' She laughed.

'He got locked up, rummaging in a policeman's dustbin.'

'Dustbin?'

'They thought he was planting a bomb. When he told them he was looking for inspiration they locked him up. Prevention of Terrorism Act. Held incommunicado for seven days. Freaked out. Nobody knows where he is.'

I ran the toy ambulance up my arm, across my shoulder and onto hers. I drove down her arm and into her lap. She took my shoulders and pushed me onto the grass by the river, and we kissed again.

'I'll always keep it,' I said.

'And I hope you do!' She wiped her face with a handkerchief. 'London was so hot. I had to shower twice a day. It's cool down here, air to breathe; last night was the only decent time I had. We went out, old friends from school.' They drank cocktails and danced with each other. The evening ended at her mother's flat, and they'd had a mad time.

'I thought about you, standing with a drink, thinking. He'll be somewhere with a glass of cider having just as good a time.'

'I didn't.'

'Did you miss me?'

'Dick got me drunk.'

'Drunk?'

'Jackson's garage. Green cider, I was ill. Saw things.'

'What?'

'Nightmares.'

'That wasn't my fault.'

'No,' I said. I only wanted her. I said, 'Can I kiss you again?'

'Yes.' She held her body close to me. I ran my hands to her waist, and a strip of skin above her skirt, where I could feel it was smooth and tiny hairs grew, and the ridge of her backbone ended.

Chedzoy let his cows into the meadow, they walked to graze at the fence. The sun set behind them, Muriel and I sat up and rested on our elbows to watch. A swan flew across the face of the sun, a mile away, towards the canal. Times passed, we were still there, a fish bubbled in the Isle, cocks crowed. The scents of honeysuckle blew down on us in the evening, I took her hand, and we walked over South Moor, jumped the stream from Whitecross to the Isle.

'Smell that!' she said, and dropped my hand to run over the grass to Bob's withy beds. She lost herself in them, and started calling for me, like a bird.

'Coo-ee! Coo-ee! Billee!'

'Muriel! Muur-eelle!'

'Hello! Hello! Billee!'

I chased her down a row and we ended on the ground.

'You're pretty,' I said.

'And you're so butch.'

'Think so?' She laughed.

'No,' she said.

'What then?'

'Handsome?'

'Ha!'

'Would I say so?'

'I don't know.'

'Believe what I say,' she said. 'Be bold.'

'Be bold?'

'If you like.' She narrowed her eyes. 'I love those eyes,' she said.

I looked away.

'What's the matter?'

'Nothing.' The withies grew around us like the bars of a natural prison, swaying in the breeze. Something moved in the grass, a bird or mouse, startled as evening shadows lengthened.

'So quiet,' she said, 'after London, it's so quiet. I forgot what it's like, sleeping over traffic. All night, all day; when I got back here I sat on the bed and could still hear them in my head.'

'I've never been to London,' I said, 'I wouldn't know.'

'I'll take you. Like that?'

'Okay.'

'Not sure?'

'Don't you think?'

'No.'

'Maybe I'm not.'

'I'd show you around. Like you did for me. There's parks, hundreds of places you'd like.'

We walked through the withies to Blackwood with our arms around each other. The sunset made the picture. I told her about my father the stuffer, and his plans for me.

'I knew he had it in him.'

'What?'

'Stuffing.'

I told her about the shearwater. She said she'd tell her mother.

'She'll paint it,' she said.

'Paint it?'

'Why not?'

She stopped to kiss me by the river. She felt me as we pressed together, my trembling knee, and my hands on her back.

'Don't shake,' she said.

'Can't help it.'

We walked to the orchard, and watched my father, standing in the yard, looking at a mangle. He nodded his head and fetched something from the garden, held by the tail.

'What's he got?'

'I don't know.'

'It looks like a mouse.'

'It is a mouse.'

He turned the handle of the mangle, and slowly fed the prone rodent between the rollers, tail first. When pressure came to bear on the body, there seemed to be a pause in time, a silence over the whole land, the mangle handle stilled for a second. Muriel and I stared at each other but did not move, and the chickens froze, dumbed. Then, with a little pop, all the mouse's insides went outside and covered my father's clothes. He let go of the handle and said 'Bloody hell!'

'What you trying to do?' I shouted. He jumped.

'Didn't see you there!'

'What you trying to do?'

'Thought I'd see if it worked.'

'What?'

'Stuffing. Preparing the corpse.' Muriel collapsed behind me.

'You don't do it like that,' she said.

'And you're the expert?'

'No.'

'Well?'

'But you have to cut them open. Not squeeze them.'

'I was experimenting! These are advanced taxidermitory techniques; all right with those present?'

'No problem.'

113

We walked through the orchard to the ambulance, and she said, 'Let's go swimming tomorrow.'

'Swimming?'

'Why not?'

'Where?'

'You tell me. Take me to a sunlit pool.'

'And eels?'

'What about them?'

'They bite; and pike.'

'You care?'

'No. Do you?'

'No.'

She climbed into the ambulance. 'Take you anywhere?' she said.

'Got to eat.' My mother stood at the kitchen door. 'Ready!' she shouted. Muriel said, 'Give me a kiss.'

'I'll call you.'

'You do that.'

16

Once I'd found a small spring, and taken a broody box from the chicken house roof, I made a trap. I fixed it so the door flipped up on a piece of string, through a hole in the top and down to a bait table. This was held from below, so at the slightest movement it sprung back, the string loosened and the door shut. I tested it on a bantam, I tested it on a stick, I tried it with a stone.

'Hide it,' my father said, 'give it here.'

Years ago, when my father learnt to hide his thoughts he learnt to hide things. Dick arrived as we carried the trap around the back of the workshop.

'You look like Jekyll and Hyde!' he said. Dick hadn't learnt anything at school. His bike was falling to bits.

'When you coming over?' he said.

'Where?'

'Jackson's.'

'Jackson's?'

'Why not? Or you still giving her one?'

'I'm not . . .'

'Won't let you?'

'Hey!' I said. 'Dick, if you haven't got anything better to do . . .'

'Hector's gone off,' he said.

'I'm not surprised.'

'Eh?'

'Where?'

'Would I be telling you about it if I knew?' He threw angry, greasy hair away from his eyes. He wore a dirty brown leather jacket, with a collar like wings, zipped over an advancing belly so it rode up into a peak over his waist. His jeans were stained with cow shit. 'Don't make me angry!' he said. Where he was trying to grow a moustache drifted a line of thin dark hair. He licked his lips, and picked at the bindings on his crash helmet.

'My best friend, he was.'

'Thanks.'

'Dog friend.'

'Only because he saved you a four-mile walk every day. You know it, Dick, soon as you got that bike I never saw him. Small wonder he took off. You've been neglecting him. He's gone looking for a new home.'

'I'm not even his master to leave. He's Chedzoy's dog, I only took him rounding. Chedzoy gave him a thrashing so he stuck to me, he was scared.'

'You want to look for him.'

'Asking or telling?'

'Either.'

'You going to help me?'

'You know where he'd go, get on that bike and make it work for a living.'

115

'What you talking about? Trying to get rid of me?'

'Me?'

At this moment, my mother appeared, to shout, 'What the bloody hell is this?' She came round the corner carrying a mangle by the handle. 'Who stained my mangle?' I watched my father dart across the yard behind her.

'I don't know,' I said.

'So you're not surprised my mangle's in this condition?'

'No. I mean . . .'

'What?'

'Yes.'

'Why "no" then?'

'Don't know.'

'We were talking about something else.'

'Shut up, Dick.'

'Only trying to help.'

'My mangle's ruined. What is this anyway? Blood?' My father walked into something. She shouted, 'That you?'

'Who'd you think it is?'

'Mangle vandal?' she asked him.

Dick asked me about Muriel's ambulance. 'That's the stupidest thing I ever saw, that girl driving around; she nearly had me off the bike.'

'Maybe you don't know Muriel.'

'Oh! Muriel!' he said, 'I don't know Muriel!'

Research into animal behaviour has shown scientists that young animals never approach their parents until after a meal. We ate cold pork pie and pickles for lunch, and fruit; apples or bananas. When the old man pushed his chair back to the wall and lit a cigarette, I asked if I could borrow the van.

'He can't!' my mother shouted. I said, 'I didn't want it anyway; just give me the afternoon off.'

'Why?'

'Don't know yet, we might go swimming.'

'Swimming? In the river?'

'Yes.'

116

'You're mad. They'll have your toes off.'

My father said, 'She's right.'

'Give me the afternoon off.'

'Tell me who ruined the mangle, I might think about it.'

'You still on about that?'

She never used the mangle. She only wanted an argument.

'What have you ever used it for? Crushing roots?'

'Crushing roots; right, crushing roots, for the chickens. It's useful for that.'

On the road to Drove House I met two hikers. They had packs on their backs, sat in the verge and leant on them. The girl wore a vest and pants. In the heat, the straps on her pack had grooved welts into her shoulders. The man wore no shirt, and his chest was covered in thick, greasy hair.

'Howdy!' he said.

Americans come to explore the mystical sights of Somerset on a month's tour away from their studies in London colleges. Malk was studying Pre-Christian beliefs. He was knocked out by the liquid quality of the landscape, and the way the morning seemed to float out of the ground rather than the sky. He wanted to take some of it back with him, something tangible, to underline the gist of his thesis; if only he could! His eighteen months in England had opened his eyes to the age of Europe and given him the strength to tackle France, Spain, Italy and Greece. Nothing though, he felt, would prepare him for Greek light. Dan Rummer had told him to expect a white light, burning the crust of America off his eyes. Sis, his girlfriend, though really we're more than friends in the conventional sense, didn't say much, except 'You're talking bullshit' every time he did. When they said they were living in London, I said, 'I wonder if you know a friend of mine? Muriel; she's from London, she's staying up the road.' I pointed.

'American?'

'No.'

'Muriel? Muriel who?'

'Wells.'

'From London?'

'Yes.'

'Millions of people live there.'

'Do they?' He gave me a look.

I sometimes feel conversations get away from me because I've something missing, a lack of sharpness, or the need to appear more stupid than I really am. I think this is grounded in a fear of rejection. I am an insecure person with a basketful of worry. If I could make a big enough basket it still wouldn't be big enough. That's how bad it is. I spent too much time at school arranging things to prove that I was bigger than what I was being taught, now I stand in the road talking to people who speak a language I don't understand.

'Howdy!' said Muriel. She noticed my long face, the hikers had upset me. 'What's the matter?' She put her arms around my neck, 'Come on, it's never that bad.' I rested against her, and she stroked my hair, and kissed it. 'Tired?'

'Not really.'

'What is it?'

'Some Americans I met coming over, he said "Howdy!" like you did, but then went on and on about nothing. And mother's been on about her mangle; Dick's going round the bend. It's been one of those days.'

'Hi!' Anne appeared at the top of the stairs and tripped by, carrying a book about drawing. 'What a day!' she said, 'I feel your age!' She looked me in the eye, put out her hands, one on my shoulder, the other on Muriel's. 'Do something today I can't.'

Carrying lager across West Moor, and following the cut of Westport canal, I saw the hikers walking north. They saw us and stopped, but when I thought they were going to come over, turned round and went in the opposite direction.

I said, 'There they are, the Americans.'

'Let's not make ourselves too conspicuous.'

'All right.'

We crouched in the grass, within the sight of Hambridge church, breathing like moths on a leaf. Her hand was warm.

'They gone yet?'

'Yes.'

Down by the Isle, the river flowed gently to the sea, eddying in pools at its banks, I chose one, passed it for another, and passed that when I saw a shaded place with willow trees, and a semicircle of reed, growing around. We scared a pair of mallard from the water, laid towels on the grass and Muriel hung the lager in a bag, to cool in the river. The sound of a church bell. The reeds, whispering in the breeze, broke above the gentle flow of the Isle. I stared at it.

'Got your trunks on?'

'No.'

'Pity.'

'And you've . . . ?'

'Got a bikini.' She stood up, unbuttoned her dress and lifted it off. In stretching, her stomach pinched in, and her navel lengthened, like lips, the soft hairs there shining in the sunlight. On the left side of her body, at a spot beneath the ribs, she had a brown mole, raised above the surface of her skin like a seed. She kicked her shoes off. Her thighs were like tropical vegetables, she walked to the edge of the river, and up to her ankles in mud.

'It's cold!' she screamed, turned round, balancing in the slime, bent down, and flicked a palmful over me. 'Come on! Get 'em off!'

I stepped out of my trousers and shirt and stood in my pants. People never swim around here. There is so much water, who would? I saw bubbles on the surface, she took a deep breath, her arms out, and dived in. Her head went under, just her bottom showed above the water, she surfaced, and threw her head back, so her hair flipped onto her neck.

'Come on!'

119

'Me?'

She stretched her arms out at nobody else. 'Who else?' she said, 'Dumbo!' What could I do?

'It's freezing!' First, the cold, then the thought of eels, cruising through the water, searching virgin brown leg, a muddied light reflected off their bodies. I walked into the river, up to my waist, holding my arms level with my shoulders, and as I began to sink, Muriel swam off, upstream. She kicked little sprouts of water, this Isle had never seen anything like it. I kicked after her, my feet feeling the mud on the bottom, imagining sharp teeth. An adult pike could take a leg off, a vicious beast, best served by the fillet, baked.

She trod water, I met her where the current was strongest, it pushed me onto her, and we fell back to kiss. It did not get warmer. Her arms and neck were covered in goose-bumps. I got mud in my mouth.

'You like?' she asked.

'I'm cold.'

'And what about your eels?' she said, 'scared?' I felt something long and greasy slither up my leg, quivering, pushing gently against me, cold, it stopped just below my waist. Muriel held onto my shoulders. She balanced and let the toes of her leg peek out of the water.

'What about that?'

'Better than an eel; but I'm telling you, there's dangerous places; these waters, everyone knows.'

'When have you ever seen anyone in them?'

'Never.'

'Then how do you know?'

'I was told.'

'How did they know?'

'Other people told them, people who'd been swimming.'

'But you said nobody ever did.'

'What?'

'Swim. I thought you knew everything.'

'I never said that!'

120

'But you've got the look about you. That handsome look.'
She pinched me and swam back the way we'd come, to the
reeds and our towels. I slipped, walking up the bank,
covered my shins with mud; Muriel said I wasn't coming
near her, put a foot up and knocked me back into the river.

I dried myself. I never liked swimming. I got dressed.

'I put your ambulance on the window sill, in my bedroom.'

'*Your* ambulance. It's yours.'

'I know, thank you. Mine. Real one still going?'

'Yes,' she said, and 'come here.' I moved over and lay
next to her. 'Why'd you put your clothes on?' It was hot.
She was lying in her bikini, I nestled, propped on my
elbows, took my shirt off again, and lay on my stomach,
looking up at her, looking at her face. She lifted a corner of
the towel, wiped her forehead, and dabbed at the ends of
her hair. She didn't seem to notice me, like I had become
someone watching from outside a window at night, a crack
in the curtains, a shaft of tempting light. She lowered her
eyes and looked at me. Her freckles were still damp. She
wore a tiny silver ball in each ear, I reached up and touched
them.

'Did it hurt?' I said.

'What?'

'When you had them done.'

'Didn't feel a thing. You like?'

'Yes,' I said, 'and everything else. I looked at her face and
a tide mark across her shoulders. I reached up and brushed
it. 'You've got mud on you. Want my towel?' I stood up,
knelt in front of her, and wiped. I could feel her breath on
my face, like a wind travels miles to gust at the corner of a
field, or a bush.

'Gentle hands . . .' she said, 'put it down.' She took my
neck with both hands and pulled, so we fell back, and I was
on top, with one leg between hers. She ran a hand down my
spine to the top of my trousers. I kissed her lips, and then
her cheeks and nose, watched her eyes close, and her head

roll back to give me a whole tight neck to kiss. Where tiny creases were in the skin, stretched, they revealed slivers of white flesh, like cracks in furniture varnish. She smelt of mud. I held her behind the shoulders, but she shifted so we lay on our sides, facing each other. It was a hot day. The moors were shot with pale yellow light. We did not make much noise, in the reeds around were voles, a mile away, a heron balanced in the sky, and came to stand by the river.

She kissed me on the chin and smoothed my chest. She smiled, tickled me across my neck and in my armpit. When I squirmed, she held tighter, took little rolls of skin and pinched them. Attack the best form of defence, I rolled over so she was on her back, and pinched her cheeks.

'You'll have me black and blue!' she said.

'You'll have me black and blue!' I said.

She pushed and rolled me back, but she caught her shoulder so the strap came down, and hung by her elbow, so I saw the rise of her breast where it pinked into brown. I stretched out to help, and she said, 'Which way's it going?'

'Is there any choice?'

'Naughty.'

'Is there?'

'Might be.' She lifted her head, 'Depends.'

'On what?'

'You. Are you bad enough?'

'Bad enough?'

'To do it?'

'I think so?'

'Yes.'

'And you want to?'

'What do you think?'

She looked away. 'The subject appeared willing and able, he just lacked the necessary, how could it be put, gumption?'

'Gumption?' I said. I held the strap, looked at it in my hand.

'Get up and go.'

'Oh! You want get up and go?'

'Please.' She put her face close to mine. 'You kiss perfectly,' she said. I pulled the strap.

'Howdy! Hope we're not intruding, gee, what a day, you know, when we came over, everyone said you'll hate the weather, loathsville, English weather? The pits. Let me tell you, we believed them, we did, even when we landed it was raining, foggy, but this, this is fantastic, eh Sis? We're knocked out, truly, we are, nothing like it back home, that's for sure, nothing, we'd have been happy with the rain, fog, whatever, just to see the place, but boy, this is something! Hey! Haven't we met somewhere before? Your face is awful familiar. I'm sure.' I slipped the strap back onto her shoulder. 'What a day, incredible,' Malk said.

We had to take them to the road at Thorney and point in the direction of Langport. They had no idea. The road was as wide as a river and they'd missed it. 'We saw you, thought we'd ask; this moor, gee, we'd have been lost if it hadn't been for you.'

'Langport,' I said, 'that way!' I pointed. 'Goodbye.'

'Have a nice day.'

'Eh?'

'You're welcome.'

It was getting late. I wanted her very much.

'Next time,' she said, 'take me somewhere shady, warm and shady. You can then.'

She left at Blackwood gate, and walked to Drove House alone. I stood in the road and watched her go. It was still light. I took the broody-box trap to the closest warren and baited it. Mother had found the remains of a mouse and matched these to the patterns on her mangle.

'See this?' she belted, holding the flat corpse an inch from my face. I did.

'Yes.'

'I know who did this,' she said, 'and how. Where is he?

'Who?

'No games.'

'I've been with Muriel. How'd you expect me to know?'

'You're his son.'

'And you're my mother.'

17

Dick found Hector, and brought him to Blackwood in a basket tied to the back of his bike. He said he couldn't find a crash helmet small enough for a dog. Hector stood in the yard and looked at me. I looked back. Sweat patched his ginger hair, he looked at the bike and whined. His tongue hung from his mouth and he dripped spit onto the ground. He walked to the workshop and lay against the wall, staring with mazed eyes at a spot in front of his nose.

'Found the bugger,' said Dick. The bugger looked up.

'Lucky for him,' I said.

'He wasn't lost at all!'

'No?' In the dry air, a swarm of insects bothered the dog. The old man was in a heap of trouble. He had blood on his hands. He carried a fork to the vegetable garden.

'He was in the building on West Moor.' Chedzoy owned a hay barn, the doors jammed shut and Hector had enjoyed a short period of rest.

'Don't tell me!' shouted my mother.

'Wasn't going to,' said Dick.

She stalked to the store shed, banged the door and clattered the mash bin.

'I'm glad you found him. Come here, Hector, happy now? Treating you all right?' I patted him on the head, he rubbed himself on my leg, and looked past me at Dick, and the motorbike.

'You ought to come down Jackson's,' he said, 'we got smashed last night.'

'Other things doing.'

'I bet.'

'One day,' I told him, 'it's your turn. A promise for you.' I hadn't cleaned the buckets. My mother slammed from the store.

'Where's my bloody buckets? You men! Save me.' She put her arms to the sky, 'Save me!' she screamed. My old man looked up from his forking.

'Coming!' I said. 'Look,' I said to Dick, 'not being funny, but there's a cloud hanging over this place. The old man's in it. I'm in it . . .'

'Why?'

'Remember? He used the mangle to squash a mouse, she says I'm his henchman. I wasn't even here, I didn't know; we watched from the orchard, but she thinks I helped him.'

After a quiet lunch, I walked to the phone box and called Muriel.

'Billy!' I said.

'Billy! You naughty boy. What do you want?'

'I thought it was what you want.'

'What?'

'A warm, shady place?'

'By a river of mud?'

'If you like?'

'I like.'

'All right?' I said.

'Name the day!'

'After market, Saturday?'

'I could come, make a day of it.'

'My mother'll be there.'

'Your mother?'

'Yes.' There was a pause, I said, 'You still there?'

She came on down the phone. 'You want them?' she asked me, in a breathy voice.

'What?'

She laughed, 'You know.'

'Half past two, on the hill?'

125

'Not a bit exposed up there?'

'That matter?' I said.

'Depends on what you want to expose.'

'And that depends on what you want me to expose.'

'You!' she went.

Saturday morning at the market, I stayed with my old man, on orders, like glue, to stop him breaking things. We stood in one of the rings and watched some cattle being sold, shit covered, cowered animals beaten into the hall, for a thousand bloodshot eyes. We found a pair of young billygoats penned in a sheep row, their young owners weeping by the gate. A brother and sister, whose parents assured them Biff and Boff would go to a good home, where the hedgerows were long and green, the nanny goats many and accommodating, and a hundred children, just like them, skipped and jumped alongside Biff and Boff. A pair of Dogmeat boys gave them the once over and a tick on their sheet; infant billy goat equals veal.

When a pile of china crashed to the market hall floor, I looked for my father, but he was next to me, holding a cheap knife.

'Caught anything for me?' he said, running the pad of his thumb down its edge.

'Working on it,' I said.

'Hard enough?'

'I'll check tonight. It's baited well enough.'

'I'll take it,' he said to the stall holder.

'And you won't regret your choice.'

'Good.'

My mother was arguing with a man about eggs. Swallows flew over the market buildings but even in the sun, a cold wind blew down the avenues of pens.

'What you bought it for?' she shouted at my father, but he didn't answer, he was by the ticket machine in the car park, stuck like a pair of scissors; his back had locked.

'I'm stuck,' he said, 'help!'

'He's locked,' I said to my mother.

'Then get the bloody fool in the back!'

I couldn't lift him. 'Keep your legs together,' I said, 'how you expect me . . .' The car park was filling with people leaving market, straw wagons and cattle trucks. Mother held the doors while I manoeuvred him into a good position. 'Take his legs,' she shouted, gripped the armpits, we lifted and laid him on his side in the van.

'You all right?' I asked.

'Give me a fag.'

We put him on the kitchen floor and I went to the box to call Doctor Evans. He took a long time to answer the phone. I could hear a cricket match on his radio, and when he spoke, it was with drawn-out words, whether I knew if this had happened to my father before. I said he had arthritis. Doctor Evans shouted, 'Where's my pencil? I left one here, I have to have one by the phone, Marjorie, find me something, it's a patient in a box.' I had to wait. 'Apologies,' he said, 'but if you come to the surgery, I'll sort something out, to ease the pain; just make him comfortable, lie him on something hard.'

'He's on the kitchen floor.'

'Is he warm enough?'

'We haven't taken his coat off.'

'And he's not complaining?'

'Not when I left.'

'Quarter past?' he said.

'I'll be there.'

Like the wind, I drove the van through the flat lanes across South Moor to Langport. There's a sign on the doctor's house that says 'PRIVATE'. His surgery is held in a building down the alley; these days I know it well. He counted fifty yellow tablets into a bottle. I looked at the clock. I was late for Muriel. Whenever I thought about her, my knees swelled and my calves felt tight. The soles of my feet burnt in my shoes, and I had to curl my toes to stop falling over.

'Get him to take two straight away, then two more

before bed tonight, then follow the instructions on the bottle.'

'Thank you.'

'And you are well?'

'Yes.'

'You look a little pale.'

'Do I?'

'I'm a professional man,' he said.

'I'm in a hurry,' I said.

It was twenty to three, ten minutes late already, I worked it out; the time I'd take getting home, feeding the old man his pills, levering him into a more comfortable position, giving the doctor's instructions, getting back in the van, driving to Higher Burrow, getting up the hill to find Muriel had got fed up waiting and gone home.

'Take two of these,' I said.

'They'll make me get up and walk?' he said, 'Our Lord living in these pills?'

'What?'

'Get me a glass of water.'

'Where's mother?'

'Catching tomorrow's lunch.'

'Here!'

I propped him up and fed the pills. 'You want moving?' I said.

'What you asking him for?' She came back with a dead chicken tied to her belt. 'What about me? You expect me to spend the rest of the day with him lying on the floor? Move him in the front room.'

'Doctor Evans said . . . Okay.'

I dragged him out of the kitchen, down the hall to the front room, and laid him with his head against a chair.

'Want the telly on?'

'Any chance of a beer?'

'Not when you're taking medicine,' she screamed, 'and where do you think you're going?'

'Out.'

'Out?'

'I'm late already.'

Late. The sun was shining. As I parked the van by the stile, two miles away a bird flew onto the bait and sprang my trap. It flew in the dark for a minute, beating itself against the box until it died. No one heard it, from a hundred yards the scene would have looked peaceful.

I walked down the hill, towards the house, a window opened, a carpet appeared, to be draped off the sill and hung down over the wall. Muriel put her hand out. She waved when she saw me.

'My old man got stuck!' I shouted.

When I got closer, she said, 'And I didn't.'

'Sorry,' I said. She kissed the side of my face. I was hot. 'We had a little trouble.' I told her the story. She found a brush and did her hair. Crescents of white skin showed behind her ears, she wore a necklace of gold wire and a pink dress.

'Is he all right?'

'I put him in the front room. Propped against a chair.'

'And he didn't mind?'

'Not much.'

She made some tea, we sat in the garden while the sun set. I had never tasted anything like it. She hadn't used milk, it was the colour of mud and tasted like burnt wood. It was Chinese, came in cups the size of eggs, but did not spoil the moment. When shafts of yellow and blood-red light bathed the moor the pools and rhines burned like huge flat fires, thousands of swarming flies and gnats blurred the view and we held hands. Hers was small in mine, her fingers even and clean. I have hard pads on my palms, and basketmaker's thumbs. We arranged to try again the next day, I left her standing in the shade of the angled trunk of a withered apple tree, while the insects burst and swarmed again over different spots. With silent beats, an owl quartered the lonely places, the moon rose behind me, and a night breeze wavered at the withy beds.

'He's no better.'

I eased him back to the chair, and smoothed the carpet where his feet had rucked it.

'You sure he gave you the right pills?'

'Counted them in front of me,' I said.

'Yellow ones?'

'Yes, fifty; two straight away, then two more before bed.'

'I think I'll go to bed now. Give me an excuse to take them.'

'You shouldn't.'

'You telling me?'

'Would I?'

We couldn't get him up the stairs, so I fetched a mattress from the spare room and my mother made a bed up on the floor downstairs. He liked the idea of having the fire close.

'You fall in that fire,' she shouted, 'and you'll get it hotter from me,' but she closed the curtains quietly, and tidied the blankets over his chest while he slept.

'Leave him,' she said. 'We can use the kitchen.'

When I undressed for bed, I could smell Muriel on my clothes, so I slept with my shirt on the pillow. I rubbed and crushed the material, put my hands to my face and looked across the bed at the wall. No shadows moved across its surface, no terrible noises whispered in that night. My sheets were warm and clean, the blankets just loose enough to let me breathe. My father snored below, my mother squeaked her bed in turning, but these sounds and the wind, gathering itself, were friendly.

18

On a bright Sunday afternoon, we met at Isle Abbots, in the shade of the most perfect church tower in Somerset, the building warm from worship, beneath a statue of the Blessed Virgin with Bambino. It's a lonely village with this jewel at its heart, like a huge stone radiator, a place visited by scholars and students of Architecture. The basket-makers have left though not the ghostly echo of their working, in the tumbledown sheds and lean-tos at the backs of houses. The Church of Saint Mary, the Virgin, Isle Abbots.

> There are few places in the county which exert such a fascination as this remote moorland church, which sits like a queen with her court ranged around her in widening circles. The closest of these is formed of Curry Mallet, Beer Crowcombe, Ilton, Stocklinch, Kingsbury, Muchelney and Swell . . . Isle Abbots is the innermost shrine, the heart and core of so much beauty. Moreover, it is the most intact. Ten of its ancient statues still fill the niches of the perfect tower. The chancel, doubtless built by the monks of Muchelney, the owners of the church, survives from the thirteenth century . . . Around the base of the tower, beneath the Virgin and the Risen Christ, the lichen and the sunlight add ever new tones to the golden surface of the box tombs, the buttresses, the niches, the wall and the churchyard grass. All else in the stillness of the centuries.

We sat on the churchyard grass, in that stillness, the sun warming our backs. She wore a blue shirt, unbuttoned to her chest, and shorts. She picked a buttercup and held it to my chin, I didn't even look at it, I pushed the hand away, and kissed her. She thought I was a bit eager, should wait until we had privacy and besides, a churchyard was not the place. I was her pupil, I listened to her, but it was me who took her inside, and at the altar of the lady chapel, watched by a painting of the Madonna of the Goldfinch, told her she meant more to me than anyone. She didn't want to hear this, I could tell. She had taught me well.

As we walked out of the village, east to the Isle, she made me tell her about basketmaking. I said it was a boring thing to talk about.

'Go on then, bore me.'

'I don't want to.'

'Why not?'

'Because it's . . .'

'Bore me.'

I told her they'd found a piece of basketwork I could have made, but four thousand years old. 'I sometimes used to think, I'm sitting in the same place where people sat four thousand years ago, doing exactly the same thing they did.'

'With the birth of Christ as far in their future as it is in our past.'

Quite. I watched a swan drift by. 'Go on,' she said.

'So it's the oldest craft, we're the oldest craftsmen. No one can touch us for what we did. There had to be baskets for everything. People couldn't gather nuts and berries without baskets, and when they had to harvest crops, what did they need? Baskets for fruit and veg., animals, bees, eggs, chickens, fish, cheese, traps, bricks, muck, clothes, masonry. They couldn't build a cathedral without basketmakers. Think about it.'

We held hands across the moor and sat by the river in the shelter of a hedge, where it ran off the field to the water.

'Life couldn't go on without us. We were needed. When they stripped willow by hand, before machines, all the kids in Somerset got time off school to help. Basketmakers were responsible for the first men who flew. Balloonists. They couldn't do without us. There's huge drawings of animals in Peru, they only found out what they were after aeroplanes had flown over the place and seen them properly, so people think the only way they could have drawn was with balloons, thousand of years ago; I've got a book.'

'On basketmaking?'

'The Book of Great Mysteries.'

'Great Mysteries?'

'That's why it's a mystery. They knew they were thousands of years old, but didn't know what they were because they were so big. So how did the people draw the animals in the first place? They had balloons. Balloons means baskets.'

'It's a bit tenuous. And you're one of the last basketmakers?'

'In England. But there's basketmakers in every village from Peru to Thailand and back.'

I didn't want to talk about basketmaking. I tried to steer the conversation to what she looked like, and asked where she bought her clothes. The ground was warm, the river low and the mud at its highest, cracked and pale. A pair of ducks paddled against the current, a breeze took the edge from the heat, I took my shirt off and she laid her head on my chest. A flock of sheep, anxious to find themselves where they were, cropped the grass.

'The Falkland Islands, where men are men and sheep grow nervous.'

'What?' I didn't know what she was talking about. She wrinkled her nose and tweaked mine.

'You're innocent,' she said. I thought I wasn't. I had had experience. I watched a wren hop down a log, hunting spiders, and in the clear blue sky, a buzzard, clean and preened in its summer feathers, wheeled over the field, an easy vole its prey, or a fat rabbit.

'The innocent,' she said. I didn't mind. Her idea of what innocence was had nothing to do with mine; she could whistle, but she could not talk. I could have been a pianist, or a speaker, but never had the chance. I inherited my innocence, she had lost hers so young she'd created a new one for herself. In that long, hot afternoon, when the buttercups blazed like stars and the falseness of her innocence was not apparent to me, she followed my example and took off her shirt, in front of me, as if I wasn't there. She wore nothing else but shorts. I had never been so close to it before. The sun bounced off her skin with the silent tones of a thousand invisible bells, and in that afternoon, while her eyes dampened at their corners, we made love. It was my first time.

'It's your first time, isn't it?' she said.

'No.'

It is private, what we did, but I cannot let it pass without the memory crying back from that past, of her sweetness, and the lust she displayed. How such sweetness could breed that gentle violence, when the field folded us in, and the sheep, anxious for their lives, relaxed at our pleasure.

I could not do it for long, I remember that, but in my remembering, think it went on longer. I pictured each moment, and it's like I have them framed, so now I cannot lose the pleasure I felt. We didn't get dressed for a while, she lay in the crook of my arm, the soft hairs on her legs playing in the breeze, the whistle of a herding farmer and the bark of his dog, blowing to us on the air of our love. A swan, flying, a cow, lowing, and the tiny rustles of the hedge, this music, and the music of the river, played at my first loving, and I cannot bear to think now 'I am alone' when somewhere someone carries the afterburn of my seed.

We walked to Drove House in the contented silence of our performance, while I counted trees, when I could, to distract my mind from what I'd done. Muriel's mother was displaying her paintings to nature.

'My audience!' she said, spreading her arms, and encouraged us to join in.

We sat down and the meaning of each canvas was

explained. I didn't understand a word, I only remember it as strange pudding to the main course. A painting of Langport was called 'Langport; a breath of immortality' and was about the way ancient places store memories and breathe them out again through stone. Muriel laughed. She held her knees tucked up under her chin, and flicked a strand of hair off her shoulder, rubbed the skin there with her chin, and looked at me with fluttering eyes. She lifted her face and licked her lips; I cannot remember a happier time. The words of the dreaming mother, the scents of ripening apples, crushed grass and honeysuckle, the dying warmth of the day. Drove House, friendly and golden in front of us, its windows open and the carpet still hanging from Muriel's bedroom sill, the rhythmic click click click of a record, turning at its end on the record player.

I walked home, and as the rooks flew under a pink sky, bent to check my trap. It had been sprung by a tiny bird, a dunnock, beaten to death by its own wings. I buried the body, and washed my hands in the river, sad to have killed an innocent bird. It couldn't have imagined that end: light, air, the trees and green grass, a limitless sky, a thrilling dive towards the ground, an interesting box, then, darkness, a sudden bang as the door flipped shut, a quick but painful death in panic. It dampened my feelings, and clouded my thoughts; I didn't want to risk this again, I'd have to talk to the old man, I could say the trap had been stolen, anything to avoid the responsibility.

I kicked the box, walked down the bank, found a pile of stones, and filled it with them.

'You won't be doing that again,' I said, 'you can drown and enjoy it. See what you think about that.' I tossed the trap into the river, it floated a while, then one corner sank and pulled the rest down. A bubble, the current swilled the spot, and it was gone, good riddance, I had other things on my mind.

Muriel. For all we had done, I remembered the respect she had for the churchyard, and how, when she pulled me from the grass to find a private place, she rounded her shoulders so her neck seemed to disappear, and with coy eyes, invited me to follow. I sat in the workshop at Blackwood, splitting hazel sticks, two magpies scrapping over a bush, the end of the day wishing night welcome. Now I could smell her on my skin, everywhere, like she'd sprayed me. What a golden time.

'He's just the same,' said my mother, 'had some soup but couldn't manage the rolls; he's asleep now.'

'He's only done something to his back.'

'But I think it's moved on.'

'Moved on?'

'He said his chest hurt.'

'You rung the doctor?'

'No.'

'You want me to?'

'Thank you, Billy.'

Unused to my father being ill enough to lie in bed all day, she worried, her alertness was dulled, she didn't even talk to the chickens in passing them to go back to the house.

I phoned Doctor Evans.

'Mother thinks it's moved to his chest!'

'What?'

'His back.'

'His back's moved to his chest?' He laughed, 'Very interesting.'

'And he's not been eating.'

'I'm not surprised.'

'Except for a bowl of soup . . .'

'A bowl of soup?'

'It's all he's managed.'

There was a serious telephone pause. I fingered a pocketful of change. My father lay at home. The doctor considered.

'Has he been able to get up at all?'

'No.'

'But he wants to?'

'Of course.'

'It's half past six,' he said. 'I've some things to finish, but I'll be out to see you later; seven thirty?'

'Thank you, doctor.'

He came, and said it was all in the mind, and if my father didn't pull himself together, trouble would become his first cousin. I'd never heard anything like it. He said we should encourage mobility, and help us lift him into a chair. He yelled with pain but, once there, seemed more comfortable.

'Walk him up and down every now and again. Try to keep him moving.'

'But I thought you were meant to lie them down, people with backs.'

'Excuse me. Would you care for some advice on the care of poultry?'

'No.'

'Then kindly allow me to continue.'

'Sorry, doctor.'

'I've some different pills here, blue ones, throw the others away, or give them to me. These are stronger, so he doesn't have to take so many. And try to get him to eat something.'

Before going to bed, I put my head round the front room door, and watched my mother arrange his blankets.

'Goodnight,' I said.

'Goodnight, Billy.'

Muriel. I lay in bed, trying to sleep but I couldn't. I watched the moon trace patterns on the ceiling, listened to the call of owls and a dog barking, miles away, across the quiet and sad moor of that memory. I thought about her, lying in bed at Drove House, warm, still. Her hair on another pillow, her body in clean sheets; that memory, a grieving, mysterious thing.

I stacked twenty log baskets in the store, washed my hands and made a pot of tea.

'Billy?'

'You want a cup?'

'Yes!' My father was getting better. His back had moved off his chest, he'd managed the stairs, and walked across the yard.

'I finished them,' I said.

Work seemed easier now I was a man, or else I was fooled by the season. July met August, I sucked a honeysuckle flower for its honey, insects came to the hedge to drink at privet and bindweed. Starlings lined up along the ridge of the workshop roof and imitated telephones. I didn't care. I tossed some bundles of willow into a corner, and sat at the bench, with my tea and a view of the orchard.

I picked at a string of cotton on my shirt, the old man came and sat under the window, with his awful back propped against a sack of potatoes, his face tilted towards the sun.

'Any better?'

'You bet,' he said, 'skin you alive.'

'I'm glad.'

'And you've got something to tell me?'

'Have I?'

'You tell me.' He ran his fingers round the rim of his tea cup and gave a long, low whistle.

'Dad?' I said, but what I wanted to say didn't come out. 'Nothing.' I didn't know the words, found a loose button on my trousers instead, pulled at it, agitated the cotton, while he shook his head, slowly to the rhythm of the gentle wind and the heat, rinsing us.

'You don't have to say anything,' he said, 'just don't get into trouble.' He lit a cigarette, we sat in silence, though the sounds of nature were all around, cockerels, a green wood-pecker, shocking the day with its call; sheep, gentle in the grass; the river. After half an hour, mother came, and thought it would be best if he sat in the kitchen, with his back to the stove; he'd be surprised at the difference it would make.

'By the stove?'

'Come on!' she shouted. 'Lit in summer, it's a luxury you can't ignore!'

In the sunny day, the clicks of a thrush smashing snails' shells, and the scents of wild roses and elder heavy in the air, Muriel walked from Drove House to see me, and sat on the bench, with her legs crossed at the ankles, holding my hand, playing with the petals of a water plaintain. Where the heat had warmed her nose, tiny flakes of skin had peeled away; she rubbed them.

'Don't rub,' I said, 'you'll make it worse.'

'What a summer!' she said.

We had met since the afternoon as Isle Abbots, and walked to the bridge at Muchelney for a swim. I didn't feel any terror, I floated, trod water, and crawled against the current to where she dried herself on the bank.

'Muriel,' I had said, 'I love you.' She'd looked up from her towelling, dabbed a string of water off her stomach, and smiled.

'You love me,' she said, 'I'll never forget.'

We'd been to Exeter and taken a boat on the river. We went as far as we were allowed, north to the bridge, and as far south as the weir. I told her to sit down when we came to the ferry wire, and stand up when I saw a kingfisher.

'They make their nests out of fish bones,' I said.

'Do they?'

'And are among the few birds which do not practise nest sanitation.'

'Quite a little ornithologist, aren't we?'

139

'What?'

'A bird watcher?' She fluttered her eye lashes. I steered the boat into the bank, left the motor to idle, and kissed her on the cheek, to show I didn't have to be eager all the time.

'You!' she said, and grabbed me round the neck. The boat rocked, I slipped, but held onto the sides, recovered my balance and sat down.

'Muriel!' I said, 'You're dangerous!'

'Dangerous?'

'Yes.'

'Ha!' She laughed. 'If I was dangerous, I wouldn't have given you the chance to find out. Dangerous people keep themselves to themselves. They wait. They wait a bit more. They strike.'

'How do you know?'

'I just do.'

I steered the boat out of the bank and back to the quay. A shower dampened the pavement, our clothes, but not our spirits. Dangerous people in the rain, and the gentle smell of a wet hedge, swallows, diving for insects, a natural world and a natural place to be.

We'd made love again, in a ditch beneath an old towpath by the Isle, on a muggy day, while grey clouds moved slowly by and we were bitten by mean and vicious bugs. I remembered which parts of her I'd forgotten, and searched for them on her body.

'Show me your back,' I said, and she did. Five tiny spots, the colour of chocolate, nestled together halfway down her spine, and a tiny white scar, where she had burnt herself as a child, blemished the skin but added to the moment. Where I had held her were impressed the outlines of my fingers, but she didn't care, picked a grass and tickled me under the nose.

'Stop it!' I said.

'You're ticklish.'

'I'm not.'

'You are!'

'I'm not.' She did it again, I grabbed her waist and took the stalk away. 'How would you like it?'

I held her down, sat astride her and with my knees on her arms tweeked her nose and brushed the grass over her face, into her armpits and behind her neck.

'Stop it, you're hurting.'

'There!' I said.

'You really are! Ouch!' I kissed her, apologized, sat down and threw the stalk away.

Another day, I drove her to Taunton with some baskets, and she pretended to be my apprentice. She called me by my last name, carried the baskets into the shop, to let me check the invoice and collect the money. She sat in the van while the shop keeper pointed and said, 'Who's a lucky boy? You basketmakers; I don't know.'

I drove slowly, proud of Muriel, while she sat with her feet on the dashboard, curling a five pound note round her fingers, round and round, until it was a tube.

'I'm hungry,' she said.

'You want something to eat?'

'Well done.'

'Eh?'

'I'm hungry, you worked out I want something to eat. Congratulations.'

'You're so mean.'

'Mean?'

'Playing with me, it's like you're playing with me.'

'Playing?' She reached over and grabbed me in the waist. 'You want playing with?'

'Stop it!' I shouted. The car swerved into the pavement, some people stepped out of the road, a car hooted. 'You'll make us crash!'

She got me talking baskets again. I had to explain how willow was grown, the yearly cycle, and the way they get different coloured rods. Buff: boiled in water, stripped. White: sprouted in water, stripped. Brown: grown that way. There are other willows grown specially for their colours, but these are rare and not seen so much. Some stuff is used boiled with the bark left on, almost a black willow, but buff, white and green; these are the most common.

'Muriel?' I said, 'when are you going back?'

'Back?'

'To London. You said you were.'

'I'm not sure.'

'But soon?'

'Maybe.'

'And Drove House?'

'What about it?'

'Your mother?'

'Yes?'

Another day, we stared at a map, chose a spot, took the ambulance, sandwiches, beer, towels, and drove off the moor, south, towards the coast, where the sea meets the sky at a crescent of pebbles, surf and sun. We parked by an old barn and walked a mile through woods, with high chalk cliffs like fairy castles poking out of the trees, rare birds, the gentle rush of the sea as it broke onto the beach below us, her hand in my pocket.

'How'd you find this place?'

'I can read a map.'

'But you can't tell from that.'

'Footpaths, no main roads, no houses, drawings of little trees; look at a map, you can imagine what it'll look like. Beautiful?'

'It is.'

'So we'll make it our garden, and the sky can be our roof.'

'An old cliché.'

'But straight from the heart.'

'Billy,' she said, 'put those things down.' She put her arms around my neck, 'Billy, oh dear.' I felt her eyes, damp on my neck, she rocked herself gently on me, I stroked her hair and kissed it.

We stood on a grassy plateau, set high above the bay, watching a fishing boat. A path led down to the beach, overgrown and shattered in places by broken land, held together in others by clumps of pampas grass. Where streams cascaded out of the crumbling cliffs and ran across the path, planks of wood had been laid, but these were slippery and crooked. Muriel held my shoulders and, in places, the cracks were so bad we were forced to crawl on all fours; she followed me, and pinched my bottom, I didn't mind.

What heat! We found a place where the beach became a heath; brambles, wild sea grasses, travellers' joy, twisted and jumbled into forests, but here and there, where rabbits were breeding, were odd lawns of neatly cropped grass, some with old fire patches and piles of half-burnt drift-wood, natural rooms, open to the sky, but otherwise secret.

She lay on a towel, I offered her one of my mother's sandwiches.

'How's your dad?' she said.

'Getting better. Walking.'

'Has it happened before?'

'What?'

'His back, locking.'

'No.'

'Unusual, moving to his front.' I didn't know if she was playing with me again.

We swam over the surf and into calmer water, so the towels were like postcards on the beach, and floated, watching some people walk along the tide line, heads down, turning things over, looking for stones.

'You've got weed in your hair!' she said. I reached up to see, but while I tried to find it, she dived under the water, grabbed my ankles and pulled me down. I came up sputtering, she was swimming back to the beach, kicking up fountains of water, laughing.

'Billy!' she shouted. 'You're so easy!'

'Easy!' I caught up, and straddled across her back. 'Ride!' I shouted, 'Ride, horsey! We'll see who's easy!' I lay down on her in the water, but she turned over and I went under

143

again. As I came back up, she pushed my shoulders, I twisted and grabbed her round the neck. The people on the beach heard us, stopped walking and looked up. They pointed. Muriel waved. They waved back.

'What you do that for?'

'Just being friendly.'

'Friendly?'

'Yes please.' I kissed her lips, and treading water, our legs became entwined. We pulled each other down and sideways. I lost my balance, she fell on top of me, the people on the beach laughed.

'They're laughing at us!' I said.

'Let them. I don't care.'

'I never thought you would.'

'Meaning what?'

'Nothing.'

'No. Meaning what?' She raised her voice.

'Muriel?' I pinched her, 'Catch!' I splashed away this time, reached the shore, grabbed my towel, and ran over the stones to the heath. I crouched behind a thicket, watching the walkers watch Muriel, and waited, her footsteps on the beach, her padding over the grass, I jumped out.

'Meaning?' she said.

'Meaning I love you.'

We steamed in the heat, and dry, rubbed oil on our bodies; she first, to show me how, then I did her.

'Seems a shame to waste the opportunity,' she said.

'To do what?'

She stood up and straightened the towels. 'Come on, look around! Sun, sea, you, me, towels, all this oil!' I stretched out to her, she pushed me back, our bodies slipped together, it wasn't easy, but we did it again in that green, blue and yellow room, while the evening came. Afterwards, she sent me off to look for driftwood; we lit a fire and cooked sausages. The sea rolled onto the shore, its distance surface shimmered in the moonlight. No one disturbed us. A fishing boat trawled the horizon, a flock of oyster-catchers cried on the beach. The trees and bushes of the undercliff rustled in a breeze so slight it could have been human breath, but the sky, though cloudless, gave away no secrets. The flames on the shore, the girl in the sand; the boy stared at his feet, the sea rolled back time. I could tell; she smiled at me in the fire light, but it was the last time she would, like that, like she meant it a little.

20

'Mum's asked you to tea; oh, hello!' Muriel had arrived with the invitation, Dick was there, they hadn't met before.

'Dick, this is Muriel.'

'Hello,' he said.

'You're meant to introduce the lady to the gentleman, not the other way round.' She leant over and kissed me. Dick looked at the ground, but I could see his eyes moving.

'I've got to get on,' he said, 'milking to do.'

'Milking?' said Muriel.

'Yes.'

'Could I watch? I wouldn't get in the way.'

Dick didn't know what to do; he mumbled about Chedzoy not liking women in the parlour, shuffled his feet, edged away and put his crash-helmet on.

'A bit ironic, isn't it? All those females providing your boss with a living but he doesn't like women in his parlour.'

'What?'

'You heard.'

'Billy?' he said. He didn't understand. 'Any time, remember what I said.'

'What did he say?' We sat in the workshop, it was a colder day, a stiff wind blew cloud from the west.

'He wants to take me for a drink.'

'When?'

'Anytime.'
'And tea?'
'Tea?'
'Mum's asked you.'
'Oh, yes.'

We carried the trays into the garden, but it started to rain, so
we had to carry them back to the house, and while her
mother laid the table, Muriel showed me the latest painting. I thought it was a pig, but she said it was a view of
Burrow Hill from Kingsbury.

'Why's it pink?' I said.

'She didn't have any green paint.'

'Then why didn't she do a picture of something pink?'

'Because she didn't have any green paint.'

'So she deliberately paints pink things green and green
things pink?'

'I think so.'

'Why?'

'Ask her.'

We ate tea in the room I'd seen on that ghostly night, with
chairs lined up against one wall, and opposite, a dark
cupboard, with a broom hanging on its latch. A half open
door had led to the kitchen, it had been gloomy, wet, cold,
now I drank tea from a china cup, was passed cakes by a
painter, sat next to Muriel. Muriel. She'd never known
what this house looked like, it had been changed, a summer
of living, two women, they changed Drove House.

'Have another cake.'

'Thanks.'

'More tea?'

'I'll have some.'

'This house used to smell of apricots,' I said.

'Apricots?'

'Smells of paint now.'

'I love apricots.'

'An apricot orchard. Mmm.'

The women liked apricots. Muriel poured herself some more tea, I put my cup on the floor.

'When I was a girl,' said her mother, 'we went to the fair; I think back and say to myself, "That was the time, that was the place."'

'For what?'

'For knowing what you wanted to do with your life. All the coloured wagons, swirls and swirls of paint, I knew I'd be a painter. I wanted to run away with them, be a travelling artist.'

'What happened?'

'I had my fifth birthday.'

The leaded windows reflected rectangles onto the walls and ceiling. A book on glass-blowing, a bowl of coloured stones, a plate of cakes.

'Have another.'

Tea at Drove House.

'Billy's got something to ask you,' said Muriel.

'Have I?'

'Have you?'

'Yes.'

'What?'

'About why you paint pink things green?'

'Oh,' I said, 'green.' I looked at Anne, she fingered some crumbs from the corner of her mouth.

'I paint green things pink.'

'I know.'

'Not pink things green.'

'I never said you did. Muriel did.'

'Muriel, you should know better.'

'Sorry.'

'I paint green things pink when I haven't got any green paint and I've plenty of pink.'

'Then why don't you buy some green?'

'Because that's too easy. An artist must make life difficult for herself.'

'I'll buy you some.'

'No you won't.'

'Why not?'

'You don't know what shades I like.'

'One minute you're doing a hill pink, then you won't let me buy you some paint because you're afraid I'll buy the wrong shade.'

'Yes.'

I offered to do something I'm good at, the washing up. I washed, Muriel dried. Anne had to go to Taunton. She had to go to the station.

We stood on the porch while the rain blew over, the sun shone for a few moments before setting, and the world became dark very quickly. I could smell autumn, old leaves and fires, a cold sink into winter, but the house was still warm, Muriel took my hand and closed the door.

'Don't you think we should take advantage of the situation?' she said.

'What situation?'

'Billy!'

'What?'

'An empty house, an empty bed, two lovers?' She pulled me towards the stairs.

'But she'll be back soon.'

'No she won't; anyway, she wouldn't mind, she knows what's going on.'

'She knows?' I couldn't believe her. I hadn't breathed a word.

'Of course.'

'How?'

'I told her. Like I told her about the others.'

'The others?'

'Yes, Billy. Come on; wake up!'

'Others?'

'Why not? Where'd you think I learnt the things I showed you? In a book of nursery rhymes?'

'No. I . . .'

'You . . . ?'

'I thought it'd just come naturally, I thought you were . . .'

'What? A cabbage?'

'No.'

'Then take me to bed.'

I'd sat in that room with Dick, felt the smell of apricots stain the floor, and we'd stared out of the window at a winter's night. He'd wanted to come back, but I felt the terror in the place. I knew what climbed the stairs. I had watched the bedroom door close in an empty house, no draughts, just a cold and heavy air. I remember the night came from evening so quickly, the door stopped on its hinges, like it knew I was watching. This room stood guard over my life. Muriel, murmuring in her sleep, her face turned to the window, I ran my hand up her spine, over where her back blended with her shoulders, I took my other hand and stroked her hair. She moved a little, tucked her knees in, sighed, Bang! The piece of tin in the lean-to, banging years ago, the sound echoed to me, sniff; apricots, stewing in the kitchen. I had looked at Dick. He had looked at me. Terror, waiting for what was coming, we waited.

I stroked behind her ear with one hand, while the other picked fluff out of her hair. I played with her earrings, and ran my fingers down the ridge of her jaw bone. The neck. I put one hand either side of it, rubbed gently, easing, pinching little rolls of skin. Her neck. It was so slim, so brown.

'Billy!' she said. She woke up. 'You trying to strangle me?'

'No.'

'What you doing then?'

'Remembering it.'

'My neck.'

'Yes.'

'Why?'

'Because it's the only neck I've got this close to.'

'The only neck? What about your own?'

'What about it? I can't see the back of my own neck. I can't kiss it!'

'No.'

'So I'm remembering yours.'

The weather got worse. A squall of wind rattled every pane of glass in every window of the place, the clouds blew open a moment to let in a view of higher, racing cloud, screwing across the face of an angry, waning moon, and then the light it gave was gone. I looked at Muriel, she at me.

I felt alone as we lay together. A pair of headlights flooded the room, twisted down the floor, up the wall and across the ceiling. We did not move. Was it the wind, or did I hear a scream? Clunk. Muriel sat up.

'What was that?' she said.

'What?'

'That noise.'

'The wind.'

'Never!'

'It was.'

'The wind?' She looked at me. 'Country boy, you can't explain everything with the wind.'

'I never said I could.'

'But it's the attitude.'

'What attitude.'

'The attitude of your sort.'

I didn't know what she was talking about. Clunk.

'There!' she said.

'It's . . .' Clunk.

'Yes?'

'Like I heard before.'

'Before?'

'With Dick.'

The orchard trees lashed in the weather, leaves ripped in the wind, apples thrown to the ground. I stood by the window, we heard footsteps on the stairs; I looked at her, pulling a shirt over her head.

'What are you looking at?'

'You.'

'And what do you see?'

'You.'

It happened again, the odd sounds, the first boom of thunder, a minute later, the room was illuminated by lightning. Muriel's face shone in the light, she wore a shocked expression, reached out and took my hand. It felt cold and clammy in mine, the glass rattled in the window frames, clunk. I wanted to get up and try the door, would it be stuck again? I moved off the bed.

'Where are you going?'

'The bathroom.'

'Wait for me.'

'Why?'

'I'm not staying here on my own.'

'You're scared.'

'I'm not.'

'Then stay here.'

'No.'

Then the knob began to turn. It clicked, a crack of light appeared, and grew as the door opened, and Anne walked in, to say, 'Half past two, gets in at five – Oh! Sorry.' I looked at her, then at Muriel, who turned her back, stood up, and pulled her trousers on.

'Thanks,' she said.

Her mother closed the door, Muriel stepped into a pair of shoes, buttoned her shirt, said, 'See you downstairs', and left me alone, staring at the orchard, the moon appeared again, framed in shattered cloud, illuminating the end of summer.

They offered me a cup of tea, but I said I was late for something I lied about, and left them in the kitchen. I drove home, the rain eased a little, and told my father someone had stolen the rabbit trap.

'Never mind,' he said. 'What's stuffing?'
'Nothing much.'
'That's what I was beginning to think.'

21

'Why?' I said.
  'College.'
  'When?'
  'A couple of days.'
  'On the train?'
  'Yes.'
  'Why don't you take the ambulance?'
  'I'm selling it back to the man I got it from.'
'So that's what your mother said, about leaving at half two; the time of your train?'
  'Yes.'
  'Muriel . . . ?'
  'You knew I was going back; what did you expect?'
  'Expect?'
  'Yes.'
  'Nothing; I just thought we were going out.'
  'Did you?'
  'Yes.'
  'Billy?'
  'What?'
  'Don't make it hard on yourself, you're making it hard on me.'
  'Am I?'
  'Yes.'
  'You care?'
  'Billy!'

'What's your mother doing?'

'Closing up the house. The rent's paid for a year, she's coming to London next week. You could come and join us.'

'Join you?'

'Why not?'

'In London? What about college?'

'What about it?'

'But my old man. I couldn't leave. And mother.'

'Say you've got to make a choice. Someone's forcing you. Choose. Your parents? Me?'

'That's not fair.'

'Yes it is. You've got your own life?'

'Yes.'

'Then choose.'

'I can't.'

'Why not?'

'Just like that?'

'Sure. It's only what you're trying to make me do.'

'What?'

'Choose.'

'I'm not.'

'You are. College or Billy.'

'And the answer?'

'College.'

'I mean so little . . . ?'

'Billy, you're selfish. There's years ahead for both of us, you want to turn nice memories into something that would never work.'

Nice? Never work?

'I love you.'

'I know.'

'Do you love me?'

'Of course.'

'Then say it.'

'I love you.'

'You don't mean it.'

'I do. I love you. I love lots of people.'

153

'I've heard.'

'Meaning?'

'You're the sort of person that does.'

'Does what, Billy?'

'Love lots of people. You know?'

'There's something wrong with that?'

'No, only you don't love them like I love you. Not real love. Like the sort I feel. I think you feel something like friends do . . .'

'And we're not friends?'

'Of course we are, but we've done it . . .'

'Done what?'

'You know.'

'No I don't. Tell me.'

'Love, made love, you know, and that means more than just us being friends.'

'Does it? I've made love to lots of my friends.'

'Have you?'

'Yes.'

'How many?'

'I never counted.'

'Or lost count?'

'Billy!'

'Then how did I rate?'

'Rate?'

'You must have a way of scoring us, like five out of ten, six out of ten, ten out of ten?'

'You wouldn't want to know.'

'No?'

'Why not?'

'It'd be embarrassing.'

'I'm sorry.'

'No; for you.'

'Me?'

'You'd be embarrassed.'

'Would I?'

'Yes.'

'Why?'

'Because you didn't even register a one.'

'Because I didn't even register a one?'

'Yes.'

'Muriel?'

'What?'

'How come someone with such a beautiful face has a mind like yours?'

'You asked me how you rated, I told you.'

'But I didn't . . .'

'I know. You're one of those men who thinks it's all right for him to go flashing it at anything in a skirt, but heaven forbid if the girl you want to shack up with's been doing the same. And I thought you were different.'

'I am.'

'From what?'

'From all the others?'

'The "others" again.'

'Why not?'

'I suppose there aren't any "others" in your blameless life.'

'No . . . I mean . . . there are.'

'Who?'

'You don't know them.'

'Don't I?'

'No, besides, I never asked who yours were.'

'Didn't you?'

'No.'

'Would you like to know?'

'No.'

'Why not?'

'I just wouldn't.'

'John? Richard? Alan? Did I mention these names at all? Maurice or Dave? Philip?

'Muriel?'

'What?'

'Stop it!'

155

'Why?'
'You're hurting me.'
'Hurting you?'
'Yes.'
'I'll stop.'
'Thank you.'
'On one condition.'
'What's that.'
'We stay friends.'
'Stranger things have happened.'
'To you?'
'No; but I haven't lived in a hole all my life.'
'Someone lend you a ladder?'
'I thought you'd given me one.'
'I want it back.'
'You can have it.'
'It was mine in the first place.'

I was so cold. I sat in the shelter of the single tree on Higher Burrow Hill, watching Drove House in the night, waiting for Muriel to turn off her light. It really hurt. I didn't want to go home. I saw some headlamps along the road to Langport, bending and disappearing behind buildings and hedges, reappearing, growing fainter, going; I licked rainwater off my lips, her light went out. Muriel. I imagined her between the sheets, but stood up, turned my back on the house, and walked to Blackwood.

22

I made four fishing creels, curved bottoms, strong leather straps, fitted canvas covers, for a sports shop in Wellington. I used Bob Wright's willow. I concentrated very hard. I did not allow my mind to wander. I turned everything I knew into the size of a pea and spat it out. I did not care. Four creels. Baskets only a master could make. Baskets strong enough to sit on. Deep enough to carry the largest fish. Four creels. There you go. Pay me what I ask, you can order any number. I have nothing else to do. It would help if you didn't want the fitted canvas covers; these are not easy to get hold of. Yes, I will deliver them. Name the date. The eighteenth? Perfect. I will be free then. No problem.

I stood at the counter, staring at a rack of guns. I fancied a Stanley Repeater. Three foot six of steel tube with a kick that might knock you into next week. A box of shells. I could load up, stalk the moor, shoot anything. With a fatal range of half a mile, a steady wind and hand, my eye, piercing the scene.

'Young man?'

'Me?'

'You want cheque or cash for the creels?'

'Cash.'

The shopkeepers wore army surplus pullovers, heavy boots, and made a lot of noise.

'How much is that one?' I said.

'You got a licence?'

'What for?'

'A gun.'

'No.'

'Why not?'

'I haven't got a gun.'

It was £340, a great deal of money; could cause a great deal of trouble. I thought about it in a pub, and drank while the barman had a bean contest with the other customer.

'Borlotti.'

'Cannellini.'

'Flagolet.'

'Ful Medame.'

That's Wellington, stranded in a sea of wind. I drove home. It was not easy to. Thursday. Half-day closing in every town. Faded baskets of flowers hanging in shop doorways. Trying to guess what would go wrong with the van, nursing it to Blackwood, sitting in the workshop with a cup of tea and the door closed. It opened.

'Billy?'

'What?'

'Help me.'

My old man stood outside, the stick he had to use now had slipped from his hand.

'Pass it back,' he said. I put a chair under the window. 'Sit down,' I said, 'you had a cup of tea?'

'Yes.'

'Want another?'

'No.'

'How's the back?'

'How's it look? He like the creels?'

'Suppose so.'

Dick lost Hector again. Chedzoy said he'd have to pay the cost of a new dog. I was asked to help.

'You looked on West Moor?'

'No.'

'Come on!'

I rode pillion to Midelney, pushed the bike down a track and hid it in a wood. The first leaves were turning, greenfinch and blackbirds covered heavy sprays of black-berry, in the twilight an owl perched on a post, watched us walk by; the moon rose, Dick and Billy again. He asked after my old man, offered me a cigarette.

158

'Billy?'

'What?'

'We find Hector, I'll buy you a drink.'

West Moor buildings stood in the gloomy light, it started to rain, a line of cows moved across the fields to the shelter, I felt hollow, like my body had been emptied.

'Dick?'

'What?'

'I hope we find him.'

I'd had such big ideas, now I walked in the rain with someone I'd ignored for someone less than understandable. But it had been my fault, all my life I wanted to hang onto anything that seemed to care; when I was at school I kept a rabbit, stolen by the milkman; when I was older I found a wounded rook, nursed it back to health, let it free, but it had grown to trust people, landed on a neighbour's lawn, and their dog killed it.

'I don't care,' I said.

'What?'

'Nothing.'

'You're talking to yourself.'

'So what?'

'That's the first sign of madness.'

'Not if there's no one better to talk to.'

'What does that mean?'

'Sorry, Dick. I'm . . .'

'I know.'

We looked in the buildings, disturbed the cattle, but Hector wasn't there; we walked to Lower Burrow Farm, couldn't find him, Dick said, 'I don't think I care anymore', and took me to Jackson's garage. In wet weather, the place was even more squalid; half empty, it was cold. Someone was stacking sacks of potatoes against the back wall, five or six buckets collected drips from the roof.

'Jackson!'

'Who is it?'

'Dick!'

We drank the same green cider, smoked cigarettes; we didn't say much. Summer had gone, it seemed winter had arrived already. I had banned all thought from my mind. I did not want to be reminded. I had thrown the memories away, I didn't need them. You can only take so much. I had taken mine. I counted the nails in a floorboard, sat with Dick.

'We've got a lot in common,' I said.

'Have we?'

'Same age. We've lived here all our lives. Do you know what that means.'

'No.'

'We've real straw in our hair.'

'Have we?'

'Yes.'

'We haven't.'

'Dick?'

'What?'

'What's the furthest from home you've been?' Dick looked at the floor while the rain came down, scratched his head.

'Charmouth?' he said, 'that's quite a long way.'

'Thirty miles?'

'Bristol. We went to Bristol.'

'Fifty.'

'And . . .'

'Dick?'

'What?'

'We're originals.'

'Original what?'

'Original non-originals.'

I drank so much I saw awful things. Every time I looked down my glass was full.

'Dick?'

'What?'

'Why do you say "what" all the time?'

'What?'

'You said it again.'
'What?'
'What.'

Autumn, time of mellow fruitfulness; autumn, time of madness, sadness, tears and grief. I didn't care. I didn't think about her anymore. I'd worked it out. If it was to be a train in a couple of days from the last time I'd seen her, that would be tomorrow, Friday, half past two; she would leave forever, thinking any more would be too good for her.

'Come on,' I heard Dick say, 'I'll get you home. I was ill, saw brown shapes and faces looked down at me, a door opened, it was raining, a car in the road, movement, I woke up a little. Another voice said 'Dick?' Dick said, 'What?' It did not surprise me. It had come to this. I could not stand, I was put on the ground; it was cold.

'Is that Billy?'

'Yes.'

'Is he all right?'

'I think so.'

'What happened.'

'Jackson's cider.'

'Tell him; I didn't mean what I said.'

'What did you say?'

'Just tell him, please?'

'Billy!' I got shook. I couldn't move. I was crying. I had not realized I could cry so much. My tears mingled with the rain and ran into the corners of my mouth, I felt my body heave to take a breath, I turned my face away.

'Billy! She says she didn't mean it.'

'Dick?'

'What?'

'Tell him I did love him, do love him, really. I really didn't mean it the other way.'

'Billy! She says she loved you . . .'

'Loves you.'

161

'Loves you. She didn't mean it.'

'Billy?' I heard her say, 'I've got to go now.' I tucked my knees into my chest, reached for the edge of my coat and pulled it over them. I felt a bug crawl up my sleeve. It would not be warm there.

'She says she's going.'

'Dick? Tell him what I said. You won't forget.'

'No.'

'And look after him for me.'

'Look after him?'

'Yes. He's fragile.'

'Fragile?'

'Yes.'

'He's not.'

'Billy?' she said to me. She crouched down so I could feel her breath on my cheek. It was warm and scented air, coming from her body, where my seed had withered and died.

'Goodbye Billy.'

23

I felt ill on Friday. Friday. I remember Friday. When I told my mother I was going to Taunton, she wanted to come, and sat in the van with a bag on her lap. She wanted a tin of Poultry Spice, a powder with the smell of licorice, fed to chickens in their usual mash, one teaspoon for every ten fowls; in cold weather a little more may be given. I told her I could get it but she insisted. I could not stop her. She sat in the van the first chance she got, to keep out of the rain, while I washed up. The old man was in the front room counting raindrops, poking at the fire, with a pile of geographical magazines and a bottle of beer.

'You be all right?' I said.

'Get on! Don't get back till late.'

'I can't promise.'

'The quiet will be a change.'

I drove to Curry Rivel and over the hills to Taunton. The roads were empty. My mother didn't have the same passenger habits as the old man, she just sat there, staring ahead, her mouth shut and her hands holding each other so tight the knuckles turned white. Rain dripped in through the roof and fell on her head. She didn't wipe it off. She wanted to be dropped off outside Debenhams. I told her she couldn't, but that I'd park the car and walk her there. I did. She took my arm, turned up her collar, and said she'd buy a tea to warm herself up with. I lied when I said I had to see the saddlemaker about some hamper straps. I lied when I said I wanted to buy the old man a book about tropical fish. I lied when I said, 'Goodbye.' I did not mean it. I would see her again. Some people do not lie when they say 'goodbye'.

'Billy, don't move the van.'

'I wasn't going to.'

'You move the van, I won't know where to find you.'

'Mother! I've got one key. Here it is. You have it.'

'Billy?'

'You can use it to open the door.'

I walked through Taunton in the lull between the office workers going back to work after lunch, and the schoolkids getting out of school. Some drunks leant against a wall and asked me the time. I said I didn't know. They called me a fascist. I didn't know what they meant. I felt left out again. I got younger as I grew older. Soon, even the things I still knew would be sucked from my body. But I did not care. I would ignore society and see if it noticed.

Taunton. Taunton has an ancient history. Shopping is a big industry. Private schools are a big industry. Rich children stalk W. H. Smith's and shoplift. Car parks are important centres of activity. If they are not being parked in, driven out of or looked for, someone is building a new one or digging up an old. Small car parks are reserved for particular people in particular cars, residential roads for miles around are lined with cars whose owners don't carry change. Traffic flow analysis is a popular leisure activity. Sometimes, one-way streets are redesigned or even relocated, so a familiar row of houses might suddenly appear where they didn't seem to be before. My old man reckoned Taunton Council built themselves a nuclear fallout shelter with an outside loo.

Taunton. Taunton is also important on account of its connection with the Great Western Railway; Brunel's big one. Brunel believed the valley of the Isle suitable canal-building territory, but never made the impact there as he made in Taunton. Taunton, where Muriel leaves the county. Trains are unstoppable. Once someone's on a train there's no turning back. The last sight of them is the one that sticks. Stations weep goodbyes from every brick, girder and waiting room.

I stood on the platform and watched a gang of men carrying a sleeper in the rain. I bought a cup of tea and waited for the train. A pair of lovers, he with the suitcase, she with an umbrella, stood beneath an advertisement for holidays in London. She nibbled his ear, he pinched her bum, they laughed. I stared at a hoarding so long the letters didn't seem like letters at all. The train was late. It was twenty-five to three; but I had all afternoon. Mother could talk to the feed merchant for hours. She wanted to know why ferrous sulphate was the most important active ingredient in Poultry Spice. He would keep her happy. I would wait. I could buy another cup of tea. I smoked a cigarette. Some schoolboys threw sandwiches at each other. I remembered something Muriel had said. A Russian writer had died in a railway station waiting room. He had been the conscience of a nation and breathed his last in solitude. His beard had been a marvel, his eccentric ways a source of misunderstanding.

She didn't appear, I had miscalculated, she wasn't going to catch the train. Never mind, it had been a change of scenery. I hadn't lost out completely. I could walk back to the car and lie about the saddlemaker.

The rain poured. Groups of people huddled in doorways and stared at the weather. No breaks appeared in the cloud. It was set. They might as well get wet. They'd have to, eventually. Groups of people thrown together out of a desire for nothing more than dry conditions are doomed. I wanted to tell them, but didn't care.

I stood at the junction of Station Road and Priory Bridge Road, waiting for the lights to change. I watched a lorry, a bus, and as my shoes filled with water, Muriel appeared, driven by her mother, swung right, the lights changed, I turned round, watched as neither of them saw me, and ran back the way I'd come.

She was carrying her suitcase through the doors, past the booking office and up the stairs to the platform. Her mother held her arm, they were talking, laughed, found a porter and asked him to help with the luggage.

I found a ticket collector, 'What time's the next train?'

'Where to?'

'London.'

'Three thirty-five. Platform one.'

'What's it now?'

'Twenty past.'

I ran through the tunnel and up the stairs to platform two, and hid behind a chocolate machine, watching. A couple of days hadn't changed them. I was familiar with what Muriel was wearing. I had felt that material. She had treated me to many pleasures. Did she feel my presence? She looked down the line, said something to her mother, and went to the café. The station announcer said the train was coming. That was fair enough. It wasn't late. The railway provides jobs. I don't begrudge anyone working on them. People have families to support. They couldn't have known they were taking her away. Many goods travel by rail; I have sent baskets that way. I'd no quarrel with them. She was in the café. I would talk to her.

I went down the stairs and through the tunnel as the train arrived. It was deafening beneath the tracks. I ran up the other side, doors opened, people said hello, porters threw sacks of mail out of the guards van and directed other people to their carriages. It was a blur. I walked towards it. A man knocked into me but did not apologize. I had a long way to go. I stepped on a damp sandwich. I saw her. She handed her mother a cup. She picked up the suitcase, they kissed each other on the cheeks. I drew closer. I heard her say 'I'll see you next week.'

'Get the flat warm for me,' her mother said.

'Sure.'

'And don't forget to phone.'

'No.'

'Just in case.'

'And remember what I said.'

'What was that?'

Her voice hadn't changed. She smiled at her mother, they held hands and kissed again. I would have had one of them. She did not see me. I was almost next to her when she climbed on the train, swung the door shut, lowered the window, and hung her head out.

Her mother said, 'Find yourself a seat.'

'There's plenty.'

'And don't talk to strange men.'

'No.'

'Or sit facing the wrong way.'

'Mum?'

'Yes?'

'If you see Billy . . .' But behind me, a guard blew his whistle, the open doors were slammed shut, and I didn't hear what she said; I was pushed in the back by a late passenger, the train moved off.

I shouted, 'Muriel!' But her mother was running along-side the carriage, holding the top of the open window, talking, her voice rising until she was shouting, but words I couldn't hear, words her mother replied to, until the train was too fast, and Muriel was on her own, waving in my direction, but not at me, though she would have seen me, just not recognized my face.

I followed Anne down the stairs, thought about going up and saying 'hello', but it wouldn't have mattered anymore, to me, or her. She had a house to shut up, my mother would be ready to go home, it was still raining.

I drove home. Home. That is what Blackwood is. My mother had her Poultry Spice.

'You get a book?'

'A book?'

'For your father.'

'A book?' I was thinking about something else. I didn't know what she was talking about.

'You said you were going to buy him a book, on tropical fish.'

'Oh,' I remembered, 'they didn't have one.'

Mother. She was the mother I had. She knew what was going on. My father. He'd had a quiet afternoon reading. The Japanese had removed a mountain in Swaziland and turned it into steel while native girls danced the traditional reed dance. The world was a big place. Nobody denied it. But I took the van to Drove House and sat watching from Higher Burrow Hill. I was not alone. My thoughts were with me. They had real power.

Drove House, in the valley of the Isle, a world hidden from most people by the way they travel. Cars, trains, aeroplanes. These ignore the valley. I walked through a gathering storm and stood at a window while her mother covered the furniture with dust sheets. The ambulance had gone. Muriel's bedroom window was shut, the curtains open, the panes of glass reflected nothing. It was a dark, moonless night. The front door opened. The last milk bottles were put out. The yard was bathed in light, a branch, blown from the

167

orchard, a pair of chairs, the mud, illuminated, then darkness.

I walked back to the van. Before I went to Jackson's garage, I sat with my hands on the steering wheel, staring at Drove House; the last light went out, I gave into it, wept, but would not cry again.

24

I lay in bed, with the radio on. I had a headache. My father asked my mother why I didn't come downstairs. She didn't know. I heard him talking to the fire. She asked if he needed some logs. He didn't. I stared at the ceiling. It reflected the sky. Shadows raced over me. The sound of the rain, the door slamming, my footsteps across the yard. The mash bin lid banging back, the chickens starting up, familiar sounds, the ones I was doomed to hear forever.

I didn't bother to start work till late anymore, I didn't care if I hadn't the money. What was I going to spend it on? So long as there was enough for the groceries and the bills, I didn't see the point anymore. My father couldn't climb the stairs, my mother was busy with the chickens, I stayed in bed till ten o'clock. It didn't matter. Dick might call later. We could go to Jackson's. I'd met some other people there. You didn't get airs from them, you could bet on it. What they came out with was what they meant.

I had had a phone call from a butcher in Bridgwater. His baskets were late. I had always been told to be polite to the customers – it was bred into me, they were the reason we ate – but I just told him to get stuffed and find someone else to make them. If he wasn't satisfied with what I'd done, he could get lost. I'd let the business go downhill. It was nothing to do with me. I had tried my best. I had been gentle with her. She hadn't been hurt. She breathed London air, I breathed this.

My mother didn't care anymore either. When I got up and showed my face in the kitchen, she just pointed at the cereal and said, 'Finish them up. They're soggy.' Soggy. Typical. She was the only other woman I'd known. She looked at me.

'What's the matter?' she said.

'Leave me alone.'

'And stay in the same house as you? That too?'

'Yes.'

'Bloody impossible.'

'But I . . .'

'Tell me.'

'I can't.'

'That girl. She mucked you about, turned your head . . .'

'What girl?'

'What girl? Billy. Fool yourself, but don't fool me.'

'Mother?' I couldn't face breakfast. I stared at the floor. It told me nothing. I stared out of the window. Rain flooded the fields beyond the orchard. She lived in that direction. Imagine what I felt like. I had a good memory. All the things we did were still fresh in my mind, clear as a bell, ringing over the moor. I fought to keep them out, it was hard, I struggled, gave up. 'Mother. Do you love the old man?'

'Love him?'

'Yes?'

She gave a grunt and turned away, wiping her hands in her apron. 'Love him?' she said.

'Mother?'

'Sorry.' She knew all about it, she had the look in her eyes. 'Love,' she said, 'is what you make it. We've just gone along, he never knew much different, and if I ever did, I soon forgot about it. But it was different then. We didn't have telly . . .'

'Telly?'

'Distractions. I wouldn't be young today,' she said, told

169

me to at least eat some bread, and went to the front room to straighten the furniture.

I sat in the workshop. I had begun to do strange things. I'd got interested in odd stories about composers. A woman on the radio collected them. Beethoven had poured cold water over his head to keep himself awake, jugful after jugful. So much water got inside his piano, the strings rusted and the hammers stuck, in the end it couldn't make a sound, but it didn't make any difference because he couldn't hear anything anyway. Beethoven stories were the commonest. Chopin ran a close second, with Mozart third. In one week, Mozart wrote so much music, that if you tried to copy it out, let alone do the composing, you couldn't finish in a week. I thought about that. The woman who told the story spoke with a German accent. Mozart had been a tragic figure in history. Touched by God, destroyed by the devil. The woman was a professor from Vienna. She had compiled a book of stories. I remembered them, they became important to me, the lives of great men reduced to my size. I even went to the library and borrowed an encyclopaedia, but in the end, didn't care.

I couldn't avoid Drove House, so long as it stood I had to go past. Damn the place. Another house for someone to rent with more money that's right. Its damp and angry walls would wait for them. Its sheeted furniture could loom in the darkness for as long as it took. The ivy on the walls and the elder trees, scratching, scratch, scratch, at the windows, and the ghosts. The ghosts would wait in their place, preening their smiles and their dead, white, maggoty eyes, scalding, unblinking. What had I done to deserve it? I tried to remember my sins. My sins. I was no longer pure.

I couldn't work. One day, I would again, but for the moment, I didn't care. I went for a walk. Simple Billy. Sweet boy. Gentle thing. Clever enough to have been at college, he just never had the chance. Fated to be a basketmaker, laughed at for his skills by people who thought it was something he'd been taught in hospital. The last of a proud line. Poor man. Hardly anyone knew he existed, what would he leave to the world? Sixty-five years of basketmaking? Working a five day week, that's sixteen thousand nine hundred days. Six baskets a day; 101,400 baskets. What a useful thing to do, all those baskets and a cracked back. Twisted, broken fingers, hands so calloused they could smooth a plank of wood.

The romantic picture of the country; a wise old craftsman putting the finishing, loving touches to his work, content in his world, happy with his lot. Screw that. Simple Billy. Sweet boy. Gentle thing. He grew to love self-pity.

I had grown to love self-pity. I walked as far as Muchelney, and back along the river bank. The rain eased but not the wind, sheep sheltered in what protection the bare hedges provided; a heron stood in a pool, swayed by the breeze, hungry.

Muriel. In the end, I didn't blame her. She had done what she wanted to do, and I was being Billy, born a century after his time, when women didn't have the same chances. What could she want from me? She had a beautiful face and the brain to match; her man would never be like me. Dick would call later, that was more likely. I thought about that. It could happen forever. What a tomb.

This tomb followed me into winter, through the new year to the spring. Spring. A new beginning. I tried to make it so. Another day. I riddled the stove, stoked it, and carried the ash to the heap. A breeze came off the sea, miles away, a flooding wind.

I stood on the porch with a cup of tea. My mother and father took up all the room in the house, we hadn't had breakfast, they were washing. The moor stretched out, here and there, rows of pollard willow, the odd cow, Chedzoy's whistle and his dog. Dogs remind me of Dick. Dick and I used to throw stones at cows. The river saved us.

Only time I thanked the damn river, but it's never been anything but a river to me.

I carried my tea to the workshop, and soaked enough sorted willow for the morning. Some people soak the night before . . . I was by the door, staring at a tree I'd planted against the wall. It looked dead months ago, but I can't dig it up, I get a feeling, once in a while; something might happen.

FOR THE BEST IN PAPERBACKS, LOOK FOR THE

In every corner of the world, on every subject under the sun, Penguin represents quality and variety – the very best in publishing today.

For complete information about books available from Penguin – including Pelicans, Puffins, Peregrines and Penguin Classics – and how to order them, write to us at the appropriate address below. Please note that for copyright reasons the selection of books varies from country to country.

In the United Kingdom: Please write to *Dept E.P., Penguin Books Ltd, Harmondsworth, Middlesex, UB7 0DA*

In the United States: Please write to *Dept BA, Penguin, 299 Murray Hill Parkway, East Rutherford, New Jersey 07073*

In Canada: Please write to *Penguin Books Canada Ltd, 2801 John Street, Markham, Ontario L3R 1B4*

In Australia: Please write to the *Marketing Department, Penguin Books Australia Ltd, P.O. Box 257, Ringwood, Victoria 3134*

In New Zealand: Please write to the *Marketing Department, Penguin Books (NZ) Ltd, Private Bag, Takapuna, Auckland 9*

In India: Please write to *Penguin Overseas Ltd, 706 Eros Apartments, 56 Nehru Place, New Delhi, 110019*

In Holland: Please write to *Penguin Books Nederland B.V., Postbus 195, NL–1380AD Weesp, Netherlands*

In Germany: Please write to *Penguin Books Ltd, Friedrichstrasse 10–12, D–6000 Frankfurt Main 1, Federal Republic of Germany*

In Spain: Please write to *Longman Penguin España, Calle San Nicolas 15, E–28013 Madrid, Spain*

In France: Please write to *Penguin Books Ltd, 39 Rue de Montmorency, F-75003, Paris, France*

In Japan: Please write to *Longman Penguin Japan Co Ltd, Yamaguchi Building, 2–12–9 Kanda Jimbocho, Chiyoda-Ku, Tokyo 101, Japan*

A SELECTION OF FICTION AND NON-FICTION

Social Disease   Paul Rudnick

Take a trip (preferably by cab) to Manhattan's most exclusive nightclub – the fabulous Club de. Here are the darlings of the ultra-*outré* New York – a snorting, 'snow'-gilded world of outrage, sex and sleepless nights. 'The satirical richness of *Social Disease* has the snap of a bullwhip' – *Washington Post*

Book of Laugher and Forgetting   Milan Kundera

'A whirling dance of a book . . . a masterpiece full of angels, terror, ostriches and love . . . No question about it. The most important novel published in Britain this year' – Salman Rushdie in the *Sunday Times*

Something I've Been Meaning to Tell You   Alice Munro

Thirteen brilliant and moving stories about women, men and love in its many disguises – pleasure, overwhelming gratitude, pain, jealousy and betrayal. The comedy is deft, agonizing and utterly delightful.

A Voice Through a Cloud   Denton Welch

After sustaining a severe injury in an accident, Denton Welch wrote this moving account of his passage through a nightmare world. He vividly recreates the pain and desolation of illness and tells of his growing desire to live. 'It is, without doubt, a work of genius' – John Betjeman

In the Heart of the Country   J. M. Coetzee

In a web of reciprocal oppression in colonial South Africa, a white sheep farmer makes a bid for salvation in the arms of a black concubine, while his embittered daughter dreams of and executes a bloody revenge. Or does she?

Hugging the Shore   John Updike

A collection of criticism, taken from eight years of reviewing, where John Updike also indulges his imagination in imaginary interviews, short fiction, humorous pieces and essays.

A SELECTION OF FICTION AND NON-FICTION

The Rebel Angels Robertson Davies

A glittering extravaganza of wit, scatology, saturnalia, mysticism and erudite vaudeville. 'He's the kind of writer who makes you want to nag your friends until they read him so that they can share the pleasure' – *Observer*. 'His novels will be recognized with the very best works of this century' – J. K. Galbraith in *The New York Times Book Review*

Still Life A. S. Byatt

In this sequel to her much praised *The Virgin in the Garden*, A. S. Byatt illuminates the inevitable conflicts between ambition and domesticity, confinement and self-fulfilment while providing an incisive observation of cultural life in England during the 1950s. 'Affords enormous and continuous pleasure' – Anita Brookner in the *Standard*

Heartbreak Hotel Gabrielle Burton

'If *Heartbreak Hotel* doesn't make you laugh, perhaps you are no longer breathing. Check all vital signs of life, and read this book!' – Rita Mae Brown. 'A novel to take us into the next century, heads high and flags flying' – Fay Weldon

August in July Carlo Gébler

On the eve of the Royal Wedding, as the nation prepares for celebration, August Slemic's world prepares to fall apart. 'There is no question but that he must now be considered a novelist of major importance' – *Daily Telegraph*. 'A meticulous study, done with great sympathy . . . a thoroughly honest and loving book' – *Financial Times*

The News from Ireland William Trevor

'An ability to enchant as much as chill has made Trevor unquestionably one of our greatest short-story writers' – *The Times*. 'A masterly collection' – *Daily Telegraph*. 'Extremely impressive . . . of his stature as a writer there can be no question' – *New Statesman*

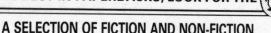

FOR THE BEST IN PAPERBACKS, LOOK FOR THE

A SELECTION OF FICTION AND NON-FICTION

Cat's Grin François Maspero

'Reflects in some measure the experience of every French person . . .
evacuees, peasants, Resistance fighters, *collabos* . . . Maspero's pain-
fully truthful book helps to ensure that it never seems commonplace'
– *Literary Review*

The Moronic Inferno Martin Amis

'This is really good reading and sharp, crackling writing. Amis has a
beguiling mixture of confidence and courtesy, and most of his literary
judgements – often twinned with interviews – seem sturdy, even when
caustic, without being bitchy for the hell of it' – *Guardian*

In Custody Anita Desai

Deven, a lecturer in a small town in Northern India, is resigned to a life of
mediocrity and empty dreams. When asked to interview the greatest poet
of Delhi, Deven discovers a new kind of dignity, both for himself and his
dreams.

Parallel Lives Phyllis Rose

In this study of five famous Victorian marriages, including that of John
Ruskin and Effie Gray, Phyllis Rose probes our inherited myths and
assumptions to make us look again at what we expect from our marriages.

Lamb Bernard MacLaverty

In the Borstal run by Brother Benedict, boys are taught a little of God and
a lot of fear. Michael Lamb, one of the brothers, runs away and takes a
small boy with him. As the outside world closes in around them, Michael is
forced to an uncompromising solution.